MW01254886

Josephine,
Hope this
makes you
Smile

THE MOVIE QUEEN

:)

Emily W. Skinner

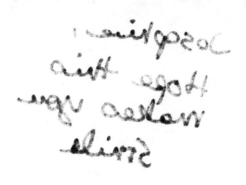

This is a work of fiction. Any resemblance to persons living or dead, is purely coincidental.

Cover Images by: Sherman Kew
www.shermankew.com

Book Cover Design by: www.Labelschmiede.com

Art references and bios are listed in the back of the book.

Editor and Book Formatter: Lisa DeSpain
www.book2bestseller.com

Hardcover ISBN: 978-1-7361911-5-6
Paperback ISBN: 978-1-7361911-4-9

For Grandma Louise

xoxo

Other Books by Emily W. Skinner

Hybrid Medical Thriller/Southern Noir
by Emily W. Skinner
Mind Hostage

Romantic Suspense Novels by Emily W. Skinner
Marquel (Book 1)
Marquel's Dilemma (Book 2)
Marquel's Redemption (Book 3)

Booktrailer:
Marquel book trailer on YouTube—
featuring actor Eric Roberts & Marquel Skinner
www.youtube.com/watch?v=6e6O7iYqeVQ

Young Adult Novels by E. W. Skinner
St. Blair: Children of the Night (Book 1)
St. Blair: Sybille's Reign (Book 2)
St Blair: The Diary of St. Blair (Book 3)

Historical Nonfiction by Emily W. Skinner
Until We Sleep Our Last Sleep:
My Quaker Grandmother's Diary of Faith and
Community Amid Depression and Disability
The Diarist: A companion book for your inspired thoughts

Short Memoir by Emily W. Skinner
Master of the Roman Noir

Coming of Age Fiction by Emily W. Skinner
The Movie Queen

Chapters

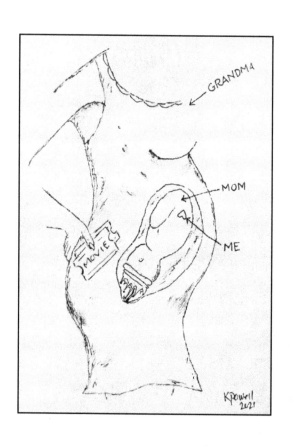

B-Movie Beginnings
1930s

B-movie—a cheaply produced motion picture.

www.merriam-webster.com

That's me. I am the heart-shaped egg in my mother-the-fetus's ovary. Women are born with all the eggs they'll ever have, and it starts with their fetal development.

The ovarian lair is where we busybodies overhear conversations, sense moods, and generally await our ovulation debut.

Mom was a baby in the late 1930s. I'm born in the late 1950s, but technically I've been in existence since the 1930s.

My egg-uncle was in another of Grandmother June's ovaries while I was an egg in his sister's. He was born three years after Mom.

Mom and Uncle Lincoln, Link for short, were Grandma's thriver eggs, the paratroopers that met up

7

with their father's sperm and conjoined to form into Sea-Monkey fetuses.

If you are unfamiliar, Sea-Monkeys® were aquarium life forms marketed to kids in comic book ads, a type of brine shrimp freeze-dried into powdered capsules that became living beings when placed in water. They are the closest representation of life developing before your eyes, a watchable womb. Well, in my child view. I'm not sure if Sea-Monkeys ever mature because most die or get flushed down the toilet by the parents of bored children.

I started as a Baptist egg in my fetal mom. Grandma was a Baptist, so my Mother was a Baptist fetus. Technically, we were all under the Baptist cloak.

In time, my mother and uncle would shapeshift into their beautiful and handsome born selves and later become evangelized Roman Catholic teenagers. So, when pregnant Grandma June worked, went to the movies, read the newspaper, sewed, attended Baptist services, etc. she was never alone. We were all there.

Legit. It's science. It sounds more like something from a Michael Reenie science-fiction movie, but it's factual. Michael Reenie was a famous B-movie actor in the classic, *The Day the Earth Stood Still*.

I didn't realize our Hollywood fascination until I was much older. Our family uses movie and television references the way sports fanatics use team analogies. Our Mother was thusly labeled, The Movie Queen.

Oh! And there will be little mention of grandfathers as I didn't know any growing up. They all died fighting *The Cyclops*.

Maybe.

These men were gone by the time I was born. My dad was the only male adult I remember, plus a lot of grandmas and aunts. We had uncles and male cousins far away, people we sought for holiday gatherings, who were not dependable nor accessible from childhood memories. The women in our family were resourceful and unique. They were a composite cast of *The Grapes of Wrath, Little Women, Gone with the Wind,* and *Hush… Hush, Sweet Charlotte.* Close. Well, distant but close.

All wrote long rambling letters as they found time to lament and drop a few dollars in the mail to one another. A letter would arrive telling of some woe. The recipient would receive available cash as remuneration for being related, a few ones or a five as atonement for bad luck that befell the sender and would hopefully not transfer to the receiver. Occasionally, a ten or a twenty-dollar bill appeared. Never a fifty. But the rare strike-it-rich $100 gift check did happen once, which was not something Mom could instantly cash as there wasn't enough money in her bank account to cover it. And, of course, she needed to send a proper thank you note first. More importantly, it required taxi fare or a long walk to the bank. Consequently, the check sat until the monthly bills rolled in. Then the deposit scramble was on, and computations were made as to when a mailed payment might avoid bouncing, incurring late fees, or prompting an embarrassing creditor call. Exactly when did the ten-day deposit cycle begin? Calculators, clocks, and calendars had to be consulted.

To be clear, Mom was oftentimes a check, or sometimes a money order woman.

A money order said: You're not cutting off my electricity or water!

A check said: *Please* don't cut off my electricity or water if the check bounces *the first time* because I didn't wait ten days to mail payment after depositing.

Side note: Creditors make charming suitors. We'll get there.

These were the high stakes and high rewards that made up our existence. Often it would all hinge on whether Mom remembered to buy stamps. We'd all hunt for change between sofa cushions, the bottom of Mom's purse, under furniture, and on any dusty surface. With the precise amount collected, one sibling would carry all the coins (the majority were pennies) in a sweaty palm, door-to-door, but never alone. Another sibling functioned as the door knocker and spokesperson. Once the transaction was complete, an argument would ensue about who should hold the stamp. *An embellishment.*

We were a lazy bunch and argued over who *had* to put the bill in the mailbox. Trash and mail were handled at dusk to avoid interrogative questions from the neighbors. "Where is your father? Why doesn't your mother drive? Do you go to school?"

Hence, the financial gifts Mom's womenfolk shared were tracking devices used to lord authority over the weaker ones and ask lots of detailed questions, a.k.a. gossip.

Which brings me to my core discipline, Hollywood gossip. Hedda Hopper, Louella Parsons, and later Rona Barrett may as well have been kin because their names were more recognizable than my aunts'. I still don't know how Mom could afford so many movie magazines on the budget our dad gave her, but I'm sure those cash envelopes helped.

Film Noir

1930s–1940s

Film noir is a stylized genre of film marked by pessimism, fatalism, and cynicism.

—*www.studiobinder.com*

Mom and my maternal Grandmother June were a contentious pair. I could never tell who started what when they fussed at each other. At some point, one of them would say something totally outlandish that caught the other off guard, and they'd both start laughing. That's how they moved on from their *Abbott and Costello* routine, but it was more like two Abbotts.

Grandmother was in and out our formative years. I loved her, but I really didn't understand her. Adults in general were sometimes happy, often embarrassing, and always critical. They complained that everything was unaffordable, unnecessary, and somewhere far away. A starving child would appreciate the food we wouldn't eat. *But we'd much rather starving children eat what* we *like.*

Nevertheless, Grandmother June was the unluckiest and most misunderstood person I have ever known. Ever. Puzzle pieces of her story took a lifetime to piece together. I heard bits, not chunks of her history, while my mother's childhood was never fully explained.

Mom was fun and had a sense of wonder, a belief that anything's possible, though she had no idea *how* to make it possible. She cared for us like a favorite babysitter, live-in nanny, or big sister. She didn't require a lot of us. She'd tell us right from wrong and advise us. Example: "Brush your teeth." Toothbrushes and toothpaste were available, but if we didn't brush, she'd say, "You'll regret it." These were simple warnings. No nagging or requirements, just the knowledge that cavities could be in your future. Either brush or suffer the consequences.

Suffice it to say, we were Mom's cast of *Little Rascals.* The *Our Gang* series of the 1920s and 1930s were short comedies shown originally in movie theaters and featured *Little Rascals*, a band of poor neighborhood kids who always got themselves into trouble. Mom grew up poor, so it's natural to assume we were her gang.

As the mother of toddlers, it was her place to be home. Women's magazines of the era provided the protocol: marry young, clean the house, produce heirs for your husband's parents, and make perfect gelatin fruit salads in the shape of a fish or an upside-down bowl.

Our house was semi-tidy. Dad and Mom were Ethan Allen people. They liked the best Early American furnishings Dad could afford. The living room was a place to decorate for holidays, dust and vacuum as needed, show off to visitors, and never use, if possible. It was the focal point of any home, a trophy room, the trophies being Ethan Allen furniture.

Mom concentrated less on cleaning and more on feeding, clothing, and entertaining herself and us until Dad got home on the weekends. Dishes soaked. The laundry stayed in the dryer until someone needed something. Floors were mopped weekly with Lysol disinfectant that came in a shapely amber glass bottle. And garbage was taken out by Dad before he went on the road, until the boys got big enough to do chores.

At about age ten, I convinced Mom to tell me about her childhood. She said it was typical. I didn't believe her. She said Grandma June had a tough childhood, but hers was no different from other late Great Depression-era children. You decide.

Grab some popcorn. Here's the short film version.

FADE IN:

Teenage June (Grandma) was the oldest of eleven Miner children. Her parents, my great-grandparents, raised cotton, chickens, and children. Jubilee June Jones Miner, June's mother, my great-grandmother, named her children after an 1899 floral illustrated wedding calendar. Her children in chronological order were June-girl, March-boy, Dandelion (Dandy)-girl, Poppy-boy, Sunny (shortened from Sunflower)-boy, Lily-girl, Daisy-girl, Violet-girl, Aster-boy, and Buttercup-girl. She miscarried November-(he would have been Nove)-boy.

A tall, sturdy, ash blonde, June closely resembled her father, Robert Tobias Miner, with his towering, chiseled features. She proudly walked with her bible-carrying neighbors every Wednesday and Sunday to Orchard Baptist services. If the Miners ran late, they'd all pile into the family truck. Otherwise, everyone strolled down Orchard's red clay streets as part of communal worship. At that time, June and a fellow congregation member her same age, Howard, were teens in love. They dreamed of becoming missionaries and traveling far and *away*.

June was a champion cotton picker. Up before dawn, she often out-picked her father so she could have sewing time with her mother. Sewing commenced when the younger children gathered vegetables, washed dishes, and swept floors. Cloth scraps Jubilee didn't use in reconstructing garments or patching were given to June to make doll clothes.

On Fridays of harvest season, Robert (with June attending) hauled their cotton load to Orchard Depot to be weighed, sold, and shipped north. Everyone in the family contributed once they were upright and walking, all but June's sister, Dandy, who eventually went to nursing school. Dandy was a rival and favored younger sibling by my Grandmother's definition, their father's favorite among the ten. He adored her cackling laugh, big toothy smile, and paternal devotion. Gregarious and boastful, Dandy bossed everyone around, to her father's amusement. Twisted his arm up to the day he died.

Story was, Dandy wanted a basket for her bicycle. She was the only family member to have a bicycle, one of Robert's want ads finds. Dandy stewed about the basket advertised in Orchard Hardware's weekly circular and begged her father from the time she'd retrieved the *Orchard Herald-Gazette* off the front porch that morning until after supper, when her father drove to the hardware store to get it. But he never returned. He stopped by the train station to help a friend move a caboose and got crushed. The accident made the front page of the paper the next day. The headline read: *Loose Caboose Kills Miner*. A Saturday funeral rivaling the 4th of July commenced with a potluck reception of barbecued meats, salads, casseroles, cakes, and pies. The only thing missing was fireworks. Afterward, Jubilee was awarded a basket of cash the likes of George Bailey's dramatic conclusion in *It's A Wonderful Life,* causing Jubilee to swear all her children to secrecy. She would disown any child who revealed the real reason their father went to town that day. Their daddy was a private man. He'd haunt them all if his Dandy-girl were shamed. This sealed June's opinion of Dandy. Her sister always got her way. But in this case, she didn't. She never got that basket.

With Robert gone, June was forced to quit high school and run what was now the chicken farm (since the boll weevil had killed the cotton industry a few years earlier). June hired another woman to assist her until March, Sunny, and Poppy were home from school each day.

Locals stopped by often to lend a hand, eye the farm, and the widow. Could the family stay afloat? Suitors were turned away. Jubilee believed she and her sons could run the place when June eventually married her beau and left for the mission fields of Africa.

With little time to think or sew, June finished her days as her father had, reading the Herald-Gazette's classified ads. It was Robert's belief that the *wants* were the best reading. Fools followed the rumor sheets. The news was nothing more than bored people writing stories grander than had actually happened, or swaying readers to think what they ought not be thinking. Opportunity was in the ads. *A man eager to unload a tractor, a plot of land, or a piano, cheap. A lady desperate to sell family jewels.* His routine was to scrutinize all the ads with a pencil in hand. He'd circle items. Occasionally, he whittled the lead point his children crushed when tracing comics. It was there June read: *Older man seeks live-in companion to cook and care for the home in New Orleans. Children welcome.*

NEW ORLEANS!

June circled the item. Her father was right! Maybe she could leave Orchard? This might be her mission field. She wrote the lister against Jubilee's admonishment. Her mother reminded her that Howard was expecting to marry her *someday*.

18

Someday.

In the meantime, Rudolf Kidson Smith or Rude wrote back. A divorced nightwatchman at the Mainland Can Company, his only child was in the custody of his ex-wife, and he needed a good housekeeper. Would June like a Greyhound bus ticket to come out and see the place?

A Greyhound! *She'd never been on a motor coach.*

FREEZE FRAME:

The New Orleans period of Grandmother June's life, from small-town Georgia to The Big Easy with Rude, sounds like a set-up for film noir. The period's films eerily were, *Suspicion, The Face Behind the Mask,* and *The Flame of New Orleans.*

DISSOLVE TO:

Grandmother married Rude and had two children Margaret Rose (Maggie), and Lincoln (Link). At this time, the world was watching *Wizard of Oz, Gone with the Wind, Wolfman, Sergeant York, Bambi, and Woman of the Year, a*s well as *Song of Bernadette, Going My Way,* and *The Bells of St Mary's. T*he last three may have influenced June's Baptist children by way of Catholic-movie osmosis. Just a theory.

The *Wizard of Oz's* message, "There's no place like home," would prove a forewarning. June's family homestead in Georgia was much like Dorothy's Kansas home. It was the place of June's desires when Rude frightened her. He, the great and powerful Oz, wasn't going to let another woman intimidate him. He'd suffered that humiliation before, so he moved June, Maggie, and Link from New Orleans and far from Georgia to Chicago—isolating June.

Once in the Windy City, he fled with the children.

Desperate to find her kids and support herself, June found work waitressing at a Chicago bar. It sounds very gangster, I know. Gangster movies were the rage of the 1940s. Anti-heroes Al Capone, John Dillinger, and Baby Face Nelson were dominating the big screen. Film titles *The Penalty, Sealed Lips, Strange Alibi,* and *Suspected Person* would resonate with June's plight.

Penniless and wanting Jubilee, June found solace in her coworker, Mike Doyle, an older divorced bartender on the wagon. He hired a private investigator who found her fugitive husband, Maggie, and Link in Michigan. Traveling with June to assist in hostage negotiations, Mike and June fell in love.

Once the unhappy family of four was face-to-face, June agreed to stay with Rude at his cousin's place (to protect her children). Mike left. Separation plans were discussed. But Rude was one step ahead and quickly parked the kids in a boarding school, sought full custody, and blindsided June in court. The judge heard the story of a wild woman who ran around with men in Chicago bars. Not only Chicago, but New Orleans, too. Rude had moved the family from New Orleans to Chicago to straighten June out. *What else could a fella do?* He had no choice but to move the kids away from June to Michigan.

Custody awarded to the father!

Rude then wrote a new personal ad to find a companion to care for his home and children.

In the meantime, the Cook County bartender, Mike, stepped up to make an honest woman of June. They married and fought Rude for full custody of the children.

Custody awarded to the mother!

Not to be outdone, Rude kidnapped the children again in a visitation ruse, which led to jail time and a depleted bank account. Defeated, he severed all ties, and moved on to start a third family. Mike then adopted the youngsters, providing them with a new identity as Doyles.

Soon June, Mike, Link, and Rose Doyle (she no longer wanted to be Maggie, her hostage name), got an apartment in Baltimore near June's brother, Aster, and his family. Her brother would have her back. His wife Myrtle was less enthusiastic.

In Maryland, Mike returned to bartending and drinking, which meant June and the children would return frequently to Kansas, a.k.a. Orchard, until he was sober. It's unclear how the ping-ponging between city and country living occurred and the duration. Their relationship ended one winter evening when June fell on the ice outside their Baltimore apartment and broke her tailbone. Mike didn't like hospitals or invalids, so he quickly filed for divorce and returned to Chicago. June's injury and his departure became a lifelong fixation and the subject of many flashbacks in letters and conversations she'd have with just about anyone.

She became her injury. June was a pain in the butt.

However, on the bright side, lottery tickets and Jesus easily distracted her. Both were saviors and could get one out of a hellish situation. Of this, she was certain.

It made perfect sense that when a Catholic priest offered Maggie and Link a chance to learn the Catholic faith, they snapped up the opportunity. Could God save June? Father Mallard and later Sister Eugenia were Rome's lifelines for the sibling pair. The religious visited, wrote letters, and sent prayer cards frequently.

June didn't dissuade her children from the Catholic faith, though there were rumblings from the Baptists. Catholicism was *out there* in Southern culture. Christian voodoo, I suppose. Catholics weren't Christian to Protestants. Protestants didn't understand that "On this Rock, I'll build my church," was Jesus commissioning the first pope, Peter, the same fisherman they respected in their King James Bible.

It seemed neither Catholics nor Protestants were clear about the folks in the upper room after Jesus died, the first Christians. Not surprisingly, all Christians claim their worship as the right way. Martin Luther broke away from the Catholic faith and his followers became Lutherans, so Catholicism couldn't be all that great. And, of course, Presbyterians, Pentecostals,

Calvinists, and other Protestants had to be an extension of Abraham's family being as vast as the stars. Right?

Simply put, Catholics were "those people" who made the sign of the cross, prayed to Mary and the saints, and practiced idolatry through statues, candles, and incense. The fact that the Pope and Vatican were in Italy, a world away, made Catholicism the great unknown, except for Georgia author Flannery O'Connor, a rising Catholic star who wrote dark narratives in her novels. Flannery raised eyebrows in her hometown of Milledgeville where families sent their crazy kin who needed to get right in the head. Not my words. Words I heard.

Milledgeville's Georgia State Lunatic Asylum over time dissuaded their wards from reading the bible. Aunt Dandy interned there and witnessed electric shock treatments. Whether the Old or New Testament was quoted, the conjuring of unwarranted spirits was not advised for asylum residents. There were too many demons invoked, provoked, and possibly choked by the understaffed mental hospital. It was later renamed Milledgeville State Hospital and then Central State Hospital, but to Georgia folk, it's whispered *Milledgeville.* You either knew people sent there, or you were told that if you didn't behave, you could end up there.

So, Grandma relied on televangelists Oral Roberts and Billy Graham to bring her Jesus. She would send them small checks, letters, and cash if the spirit moved her.

Television opened doors that kept her closed inside. *Texaco Star Theater, I Love Lucy, The Red Skelton Show,*

The Jack Benny Show, Amos 'n' Andy, The Lone Ranger, Hopalong Cassidy, and Your Show of Shows were good company.

Grandma June met her third husband, Richard Wrinkle, a Census taker, when he knocked on her Baltimore rowhouse door, just as Oral Roberts proclaimed from her small black and white television, "You have an angel, a personal guardian angel…" Startled, June answered her door. A jovial round man with damp gray hair, horn-rimmed glasses, and a strip of bottom teeth that looked like a weathered picket fence introduced himself. Would she kindly answer his Census questions and if possible, spare him a glass of cold water? She would.

He was unlike anyone she knew. Richard Wrinkle repeated everything she said, reframed as, "You say…" whatever she just said. For example, "That's a nice tie, Richard." He'd say, "You say, that's a nice tie." Then he'd genuinely laugh. She'd laugh. Instant attraction. Not only did Richard Wrinkle listen, but he provided validation. He knew exactly what she said!

Rose and Link tried in vain to dissuade their mother from dating him. Instead, she married him two months into their courtship.

Was Richard the answer to their prayers? *Maybe.*

Richard didn't drink, paid their rent, and even provided them a small allowance. It wasn't until June and Richard had their first real argument that his reverberation lost all its charm. He shouted, "You say, THE HELL! You say, YOU'RE A DURN FOOL! You say, STOP SAYING WHAT I'M SAYING!" Then he'd stormed off to his mother's house for several days. That was how he dealt with confrontation. June could relate.

Six months into their nuptials, Richard's mother died. At which point, the well ran dry and creditors came a-knocking. One such collection agent was a Polish man named Mazur Sarkowski. He was dispatched when Richard stopped making payments on their new furniture.

Unbeknownst to Rose, she was the cushion that bought them time. Mazur was thirty to Rose's nineteen and the first to compare her features to Monaco's new Princess, the film star Grace Kelly. Mazur enjoyed long talks with Rose on the front steps of the Wrinkle's brownstone, and aspired to date Rose once the Wrinkle account was settled. But Mazur soon lost patience, as Richard seemed to mock everything he said. Soon their cushions and all new furnishings were repossessed. Rose's Uncle Aster delivered an old sofa, two single beds, an army cot, along with a card table set at the urging of his wife Myrtle. Myrtle was not about to have her sister-in-law's family move in with them.

Since Richard was a seasonal employee between Christmas tree sales, summer camp counseling, city directory delivery, and parade clean-up, June, Rose, and Link had to look for work. June encouraged Rose to audition for a suntan product commercial. The winner would tour the country as a spokesmodel and appear in print ads, as well as take home a brand-new RCA color television set. Rose loved the idea. June wanted the color television. And Richard thought he'd tag along with Rose to see if the event needed a registrar, to which June said no! Link was sent to look out for his sister—with no resistance.

The audition resembled a beauty contest. Rose and 300 other women tried out for the Spray Tan tanning lotion commercial competition. All candidates walked the runway of a Baltimore hotel ballroom in bathing suits and recited a jingle for the judges. Character actor Jack Carson was one of the judges. Very handsome by Rose's definition, she remembered Carson's radio program she'd listened to while doing menial chores at boarding school. She'd also seen him in *A Star Is Born* with Judy Garland.

Finishing number six of the top ten finalists, Rose was happy to receive a consolation prize of Spray Tan products just for participating. And thus began her fascination with movie magazines. She was eager to pick up *Silver Screen* and *Photoplay* at the nearest newsstand to see if there were more stories about Jack Carson. She had to know everything about him! Was he married? Did he have children? Was he friends with Elizabeth Taylor?

The realization that she was almost the face of a major brand gave Rose the confidence to apply for a jewelry clerk position at J.D. Bradford's department store. Though she lacked the required sales experience, she figured all they could do was not see her. But they did see her. She sold them on *why accessories made even a minimal wardrobe as vast as the stars,* landing her dream job! It was there that she met her dream man, Frank Knight, my dad, a handsome practicing Catholic in the company's credit department.

A serious company man, Frank vowed not to fraternize with any female employees, especially not the gorgeous Rose Doyle. It was company policy. Being an assistant manager in the store's finance department, a man of ethics fresh from four years in the Army, he would not flirt with the beauty who was setting division records in jewelry sales. However, he could occasionally stop by her department and say hello. Or sit near her in Bradford's luncheonette to get a whiff of her Tabu perfume. Of course, there was absolutely no problem with socializing at company sponsored events. But that was all!

Until he saw her bowling with other employees at Ball-T-More Bowling a mile from the store. He was in a management league; she was there with clerks. Enamored by Rose's approach to the lane, an almost curtsy and release of the bowling ball, her curves and the curve she spun each time she tossed the bowling ball made him dizzy. Her consistent counterclockwise spin provided her a spare at nearly every approach. *What couldn't this woman do?*

In the interim, Frank ran a credit report on Rose and her mother only to discover Rose had a balance due, and her mother had stiffed the company. Scandal of scandals! Could these women stain his reputation, career, and future? But months later, Frank succumbed to clandestine bowling with Bradford's Top Jewelry

Saleswoman on non-league nights, determined to retire her, clean up her and her mother's credit, and live happily ever after!

ROLL CREDITS

Mom said that was the abbreviated version of her childhood and how she met Dad. There was nothing normal about it! A bit long-winded and rambling, I'll admit. But she felt this would satisfy my persistent need to know. I had a lot more questions.

Ok, it's time to clean the theater. You need to move on to the next chapter to find out what happens next.

Theatrical Release

1950s

The theatrical version of a movie is the one that was originally shown in theaters.

-movies.stackexchange.com

Within a month of marrying, Rose and Frank consulted a doctor about their lack of offspring. They were on a mission. After all, Rose had to quit J.D. Bradford's per their fraternization policy. She needed children to tend to while Frank worked, as she was officially a housewife and Frank a breadwinner. What else would she do all day? Of course, catch a movie, grab a sandwich at a luncheonette, window shop, and read *Silver Screen*, but in between? Their doctor reassured them that with practice, they would be successful. Four months from their honeymoon, the first Sea-Monkey was formed.

In time, we eggs made our way into the world as natural-born people. My older egg-brother Franky, Sea-Monkey number one, was in his developmental phase as our parents watched *Moby Dick, Around the World in 80 Days, Lust for Life, Invasion of the Body Snatchers, Forbidden Planet, The King and I, Bus Stop, and The Ten Commandments.* This lineup would encourage fetal Franky to consider seafaring world travel and to keep in mind that he shares the planet with artists, aliens, and royalty. And, as such, to have a sense of humor and respect for others.

Franky nearly killed Mom, or perhaps it was the obstetrician. A vein burst or ruptured while she was giving birth. It was determined that Rose had weak veins. Thankfully, there were pints of blood available, and she survived. Plenty of us eggs were hopeful. It was the late 1950s when doctors put young mothers down—I mean, put them into a twilight sleep to pull their baby out with forceps and then congratulate the sequestered father. Everyone would have a cigar with dad and the tong-grabbing physician, toasting another successful delivery when the mother *lived*. She had the easy part: lying flat on her back in an anesthetic haze. Gosh, darn those knucklehead doctors!

Soon the newlyweds had a prized male heir and a Bradford's promotional transfer to Alabama. Determined to fill their newly rented one-bedroom Montgomery apartment with small people, Frank and Rose made Sea-Monkey number two, me. Upon my arrival, they realized they needed more space and debt.

Spotting a quaint one-story two-bedroom house for sale in their cozy Westlake neighborhood, the Knights became homeowners.

The little house, as they referred to it, was a place where Rose could care for babies, eat barbecue, and watch movies while her husband was on the road managing the credit business of J.D. Bradford in the southeastern United States.

Have stroller, will travel. Rose, a city girl with country roots, understood public transportation and the expense of it. Her feet could get her anywhere, which was one square mile from the back door of her house to everything. The community bank had purchased an empty lot behind the little house and paved it for additional parking that never received much use. Well, not by bank customers, but it was a nice shortcut for Rose to Blaze Bar-B-Q, three blocks away, and more importantly, The Palace Movie Theater several blocks in the other direction. Also close were a neighborhood grocer, Rexall Pharmacy, the pediatrician's office, retail apparel, and every needful thing this mother of babes required. Since Mom didn't drive, she relied on her community, the West Lake business owners. They were all on a first name basis. She'd wave. They'd wave. Talk with us kids. Tell us to be good for our momma. Give us a lollipop.

Rose frequented movies with her tots if a teenager couldn't take over for a few hours. Frank, Jr. was her companion to see *The Pit and the Pendulum.* Franky saw his first horror film in theatrical release at three years old. One for the baby book. Only my sister could boast a more remarkable film experience at the tender age of two weeks. But she's still an egg at this juncture.

My younger brother became a Sea-Monkey when I was five months old. His birth required Mom to have yet another blood transfusion. His name is Clark Miner Knight (as in Clark Gable), which Dad only agreed to because Mom was weak. He refused to have his children named for movie characters, but actors were the exception. I am named for my paternal Grandmother, Everly, who was named for her paternal Grandmother, Everly. My nickname, Omelet, solidified my egg identity. The parents also called me Tweety-Bird because I had a big head and a sprig of hair. However, I looked more like Curly from the *Three Stooges*.

Eventually, Dad would want to invest in a bigger house in a newer neighborhood, which would become Montgomery abode #3. Anyway, a bigger house meant a tighter budget. To keep their growing trio strong, the parents used powdered and bottled milk to stretch their food budget. Mom liked chocolate milk, too, said it was good for her stomach. Anyway, one especially rambunctious afternoon, with three little ones scream-ing repeatedly chocolate milk. Mom repeated back, "You want chocolate milk? You want chocolate milk?"

We cried, "Chocolate milk!"

To which she poured over it our heads. I think she really enjoyed it, too. It was the boldest move I ever recall her making.

Franky and I were a pair of mischief-makers. I was the instigator, the bossy child. Franky was the darling. Poor Clark was in our crosshairs. We eventually blamed everything on Clark because no one punished a baby. But Mom was on to us. She was not a disciplinarian and always tried reasoning with us or waiting us out. The chocolate milk shrieks had been her breaking point.

As for the street we moved to, it had cinematic significance. Orson Wells wasn't the only one with a Rosebud. We moved to Rosebud Lane when I finally had a full head of hair, a growing imagination, and an appreciation for fine art, fine art as in when Dad decided to paint fancy numbers on our mailbox.

Franky and I watched. Crouching down, jumping, reaching for the paint, offering to help, and asking lots of questions. Stepping back as requested. We were not allowed to touch anything but dared to do so.

Dad painted the number two.

Ecstatic, I declared, "That's a chicken!"

My brother said I was uninformed. He clarified I was witnessing Mailbox ABCs.

Franky was silly.

"It's a chicken," I repeated.

Franky rolled his eyes.

Dad painted the number 4.

"That's a boat!" It was so obvious. You couldn't miss it.

Franky shook his head.

Dad continued to work his brush into the paint and define the numbers.

Franky really needed a mini smoking jacket and pipe between his teeth as he continued his dissertation on alphabet learning of which I, too, would someday undertake. He cleared his throat. Indeed, "Mailbox ABCs."

"It's a boat," I said. Jumping up and down and waiting for the next stroke of the master's brush.

Dad painted the number 8.

I yelled, "That's a rubber band!"

"NO!" Franky flailed on the lawn. *Tweety Bird may have hair, but she's not learned her ABCs! Would Dad please tell the giggler!* "Dad!"

Dad winked at me.

I was unwavering. Making my own figure eight around the mailbox and Franky, I shouted, "It's a chicken, a boat, and a rubber band! A chicken, a boat, and a rubber band! Chicken, boat, and rubber band!"

I need to get Franky a snow globe with a mailbox inside to commemorate 248 Rosebud Lane.

Mom said the Rosebud house was too big for us. I remember little, except that the basement collapsed shortly after we moved in. We weren't allowed to go into the basement. Well, except for Clark. He fell down the basement stairs several times, opening the wrong door while looking for Mom in the middle of the night.

Come to think of it, it was a bit of a dangerous place. The house was on a hill. Outdoor activities were a vertical challenge for us. Clark would attempt feats of heroism by running his toddler legs as fast as they could go down our driveway to catch my baby doll stroller. Sometimes it escaped my grip, *sometimes on purpose.*

It was funny watching Clark go. Thankfully all rolling commenced in the grass. I even ripped my tiny right thumb trying to slide down our wrought iron railing. I still have the scar.

There was a neighbor boy who babysat us when Mom went bowling. His name was Bubba, but we called him Bubbles. Mom and Dad had expanded their Ethan Allen collection to bedroom furniture. I chewed on the dresser corner while begging Mom to not go out. I can still taste the varnish and see the scraped finish. I'd chew. She'd put on her bowling socks. I would cry and gnaw. She told me be she'd be back. She and Carla were only going to be gone a little while.

Carla was her only friend on the block, a shapely Italian woman with a tall black bouffant that ended with a stiff upside-down question mark ponytail that looked like a snake resting on her collarbone. Carla was unlike any woman Mom knew. Well, in my child view. She and Carla were friends for a fleeting time. Carla's husband, Sonny, a heavy cologne wearer in a black leather jacket and a five o'clock shadow, visited Mom a few times to corroborate his wife's alibi. He was a pudgy Frankie Avalon type. Was Mom *with* Clara the night of? Mom realized she was a smokescreen for her fellow bowler on non-bowling nights. Sonny came by a several times feeling lonely, looking for his Carla and/or some feminine consolation. That ended Mom's bowling career!

Mom's only other friend was another J.D. Bradford's wife, Yvette. Yvette's husband and Dad were young executives at the time. Yvette and Burt Samson had a son Bobby who was about Clark's age. We all played together while our mothers talked. Talking doesn't really describe it. It was way longer than talking. It was motherly conceptualizing—dizzying theories about men, celebrities, Jackie Kennedy, the president, interior decorating, Bradford's sales, mayo versus Miracle Whip. Their discussions could go on for days if one of us didn't hit each other and break up their conversation.

Yvette copied everything Mom did. She bought the same furnishings, identical boys' clothes, movie magazines, crochet thread, and afghan patterns. That's what tipped me off. Yvette's afghan had one square that stood out like a *Highlights magazine* puzzle. What's wrong with this picture? I pointed it out to my Mom. The afghan was stretched across Yvette's sofa with one brown square where there was no brown square on our afghan at home. Mom informed me that Yvette ran out of yarn. Except for that one square, our house and Yvette's were nearly the same. The matchy-matchy was a pet peeve of Mom's. She was flattered and annoyed. Hardly a fault, however I remember it. But since Yvette was also our ride, Mom bit her tongue. She had yet to branch out on her own. There were public transportation options but navigating three kids was still fresh territory. It was probably a good thing for us that Mom was dependent for rides. Jumping off at a wrong bus stop would have been in the cards for one of us. Thankfully, Bradfords' wives supported one another.

Television replaced movies for a time unless Mom and Dad went out on *his* weekends home. Dad drove a multi-state territory all week long and didn›t want to go anywhere when he got home. Mom, tired of multi-child herding all week long, wanted a night on the town when Dad got home. It was an ongoing struggle. Their romance waned at times.

Instead, Mom and Dad settled on nights in front of the television with TV dinners until it was time for him to leave again. Mom's companions during the week were *Bachelor Father, Perry Mason, The Real McCoys, Leave It to Beaver, Tonight Starring Jack Parr, Father Knows Best, Alfred Hitchcock Presents, Gunsmoke, Have Gun—Will Travel, Zorro,* and *Lassie.*

Itching to see and do more, Rose needed a passion that would take her places, places she longed to explore. She found a solution in her magazines: books by mail. She could build her own library! Dad agreed. Book-of-the-Month Club, Reader's Digest Condensed Books, and later Literary Guild subscriptions would add to her reading repertoire.

Books gave Mom the intellectual stimulation she needed to elevate her and Dad's conversations. Dad even enjoyed packing a book or two for his week. Their collection included the classics, biographies, popular fiction, and world religions. Both wanted to learn more about other faiths. They also had a mutual curiosity for history, notably Abraham Lincoln and the Civil War. I can barely remember them being together long enough to discuss the books they read, but I remember the excitement of book boxes. I didn't know Dad's political preference, but as a businessman, I got the vibe that he always disagreed with the day's news. Mom loved JFK and Jackie, the Camelot era in the White House. The Kennedys were good Catholics, and we were Catholic. So, the Kennedys were our people. Well, at least to Mom.

Not that we were great Catholics; we were just Catholic. Since Dad traveled so much, it was hard for us to get to Mass on Sundays. He wanted to sleep in, but he was also our Sunday School transportation. On the Sundays that we made it to evening Mass, *Voyage to the Bottom of the Sea* permitting, Dad would linger by the television, stalling. Mom would get us all in the car. Dad would emerge five minutes later and drive leisurely to the church.

They would discuss how much time it would take to get to church. God forbid you'd walk in after the Gospel reading because it didn't count if you did. Every good Catholic knew not go in to Mass if it wasn't going to count in the eyes of God. When we finally got there, Dad would pull up, motor running. He'd look at his watch and calculate the time it would take to park and walk in. I was calculating his calculating. He and Mom would begin heated muttering. I would look out my window, knowing God wanted us in church.

"Are we going in?" I'd say.

My brothers would shrug. I was unconvinced our walking in late was as offensive as discussing it in the parking lot. Dad'd drive off. Foiled again. Gospel timing! The parents would assure us that next week we'd leave the house earlier.

How were we going to make our First Communion if we didn't go to Sunday School or Church? They devised a plan. Mom would get us kids up earlier, feed and dress us. Then she'd stay home and get dressed while Dad made the Sunday School run. Once Sunday School drop off was over, Dad would pick Mom up, then they'd pick us kids up, and we'd all go to Mass. The difference between what we usually did and the new plan was them convincing themselves it was different.

I cannot remember being signed up for religious education. When Dad did drop us off, it was after everyone was in class. We were clueless as to where to go or what to do. He just dropped us off and assumed the nuns would oversee everything. They didn't.

On second thought, maybe they did. Our individual teachers, lay people, other kids' parents, would quiz each of us on any number of things: from our name, address, and phone number, to where and who our parents were, and can you say the *Hail Mary* and the *Our Father*.

We knew the *Hail Mary* and *Our Father* better than we knew where we lived. Mom expected Dad to manage all things Sunday School. Both wanted the other to be the responsible one. They had committed to our religious upbringing when they got married. It's a Catholic thing: have children, raise them Catholic, and hopefully, a few will become priests or nuns. The local church counted on their engaged couples to understand they were repopulating future vocations in the United States dioceses. The numbers should work in the Vatican's favor, knowing the Holy Spirit would take care of the everything if the kids simply got to Sunday School and Mass!

The grind of getting up early on Sundays was not in Dad's wheelhouse. Instead, he purchased a *Baltimore Catechism,* determined to teach us himself. Classes were held in the boys' bedroom. We were to be quiet, still, and listen. This was vastly different from our weeklong romps, fighting over toys while Dad was on the road. Mom was adamant about our being quiet when Dad was home. So, we didn't say a word during his lessons. We didn't necessarily understand it, either. It was like a foreign language. I focused on my brothers fidgeting. I, too, wondered how long these classes would take. Dad would read, read, read, and look at us. We'd stare back. Then he'd give us a catechism quiz. We'd shrug.

Dad got frustrated and asked, "What did they teach you in Sunday School?"

Nothing. We barely went.

His catechism lessons halted before they ever really started. Church of the Incarnation mysteriously accelerated the process of our First Communion. Franky and I received our sacraments together. I should have been a year behind him. I guess they decided to get two out of the way. Jesus, Mary, and/or Joseph interceded I suppose? Or maybe the parish understood Mom's story. She was a non-driving convert with three clueless kids and an exhausted husband. She needed a miracle. Or wait a minute... Mom wrote the Bishop in Baltimore! It must have been Mom's friendship with the newly promoted Bishop Mallard, who called in a favor to his brethren in our local diocese. Sounds downright Marlon Brando in the *Godfather*. I've underestimated the power of influence.

Mom had connections, powerful connections who understood her sincere effort to potentially add to church vocations. Was there a future Knight priest or nun residing in her household? The bishop had made a way. Mom was relieved. She didn't want to teach us anything that could be graded or measured. She had less education than Dad. Even though she was book smart, street smart, as well as poised and design-focused, she didn't have the confidence to tutor what she thought more intelligent people should.

Rose understood her limitations. Well, it was more like her lack of a diploma that caused her to doubt herself. Where she really excelled was her personal style. She was a looker. Men stared at her. Clerks held up lines to chat with her. Other women asked where she shopped. She advised her admirers to buy expensive over cheap. Classic styles would always be in fashion over last year's fad. Her wardrobe consisted of a few: dresses, skirts, hats, blouses, brooches, faux pearls, oversized Hollywood sunglasses, and plum pink lipstick. A bona-fide hat woman, she could easily do a pillbox throwdown with Jackie Kennedy any day. My favorite hat was her aqua-feathered Cloche from Sears. She hid the hat box because it disturbed Dad that she bought from the competition. The only Chanel she could ever afford was No 5.

When Mom gained weight, Dad and the grand-mothers told her. The social attitude of the day was to shame women into weight loss. Men were under-standably large and could carry a few extra pounds, but even they could find themselves in the bull's eye. Fat jokes were the norm on comedy albums and tele-vision acts. It was an unkind era. Flaws, whether it was a woman's weight, a man's ability to put food on the table, if children were well-dressed and behaved, or just about anything related to the home was common fodder. Your house was either too big or too small. Your television was either a color console with a radio and stereo or a flimsy black-and-white model with rabbit ears. You know, the important stuff. A nosy neighbor would ring your doorbell with authority. No sooner had you opened the door than she'd push her way in with a guise of concern. "Your kitchen is downstairs? How odd. Why?"

Mothers were stay-at-home bored. Fathers were tired and needed a little Geritol, even at age 30. Children roamed their and other peoples' neighborhoods by foot or bicycle and only came home when hungry or called. Family, in our case, was the aunts or grandmothers who moved in for extended stays called visits.

We were suburbanites, the prosperous emerging middle class. Dad was a Kent man. He smoked reg-ulars, not menthols, from age 14. Secondhand smoke had not been invented then, so everyone smoked freely wherever and whenever. I remember gazing at the elegant soft pack of Kent cigarettes that occasionally graced our countertop. They were otherwise in his white shirt pocket. These were the Cary Grant of cigarettes. A thin pinstripe ran horizontally through the off-white pack where the word KENT loomed large under a small castle emblem. An official stamp sealed the top edge. A cigarette to aspire to.

Mom didn't smoke and said it wasn't ladylike. Grandma June did. She had a talent for talking with a cigarette stuck to her lips. It was totally distracting and hypnotic. You'd focus so much on the cigarette bouncing up and down as she talked that you'd have no idea what she was saying. Every now and then, she'd look at me and laugh. My staring was that obvious. Grandma had a pretty smile, a relaxed throaty chuckle, plus a distinct Georgia dialect. She and my Great Grandmother Jubilee could have written country and western songs.

Like: "I don't nuther." It would go like this: "What you think about them politicians? I don't like 'em. I don't nuther."

Or this classic: "That ole…." "That ole fella's a darn fool. That ole raccoon et all the corn. That ole mailman's never on time."

But Grandma June could've have put Patsy Cline's *Crazy* to shame with "The hell."

Think "what in the hell," but shorten it to "the hell."

You ignored Grandma calling you. She'd say, "The hell."

Mom would tell Grandma June you didn't hear her, and Grandma'd say, "THE HELL!"

Dad would come home a day early from a week's travel while Grandma was still visiting. And she'd mutter, "The hell."

As for our diet, I remember Chef Boyardee® pizza kits, SpaghettiOs®, canned fruit and vegetables, cream corn, apple sauce, instant mash potatoes, meatloaf, fried baloney, TV dinners, Spam®, Underwood® Deviled Ham, Libbys® Vienna Sausage, StarKist® Tuna, sloppy joes, southern fried chicken, and country-fried steak in the cast iron skillet, roast beef and potatoes in the pressure cooker only on Sundays, sliced tomatoes and cucumbers, American cheese slices, mayonnaise sandwiches, sugary cereals, bananas or peaches and cream (sliced fresh bananas or peaches sprinkled with sugar, floating in milk), Jiffy pop® Popcorn, Jell-O®, and Hershey®'s bars. I didn't see a salad other than coleslaw until the 1970s. Everything was about convenience. Healthy eating hadn't been invented then. It was more important to have your meal prepared quickly and on a TV tray before your favorite television show started.

We drank white milk, chocolate milk, and Kool-Aid®. Sodas came along later: Fresca®, Tab®, Coke®, and Canada Dry® Jamaica Cola. We didn't drink water unless it was out of a yard hose or a public water fountain.

On Fridays, we Catholics ate fish. They were frozen fish sticks baked to the point of drying out the small amount of fish that existed in the heavily breaded variety unless Dad was home and picked up takeout from a local seafood place, The Shrimp Boat. At these times, I only ate hush puppies. I also enjoyed mashed potatoes and apple sauce together. My brother Franky liked to eat Jell-O® painstakingly slow to irritate Clark and me, who gobbled ours.

The parents didn't take us out to eat other than White Castle® or Huddle House® unless it was a special occasion. Then we'd go to a sit-down restaurant. I wasn't a fan of those little burgers from White Castle. Dad and Mom enjoyed the semi-crunchy onions and mustard that came on them. We were told you couldn't get them with ketchup or without onions. We learned to tolerate mustard and onions and eventually developed a taste for them. Well, I did.

Mom loved onions. She could eat a Vidalia onion like an apple. She was also known to chug juice from the pickle jar and buy sausage out of those mysterious red liquid-filled jars at neighborhood stores. She was a pickled woman!

Montage

⧗

1960s

The montage is most frequently used to speed up the time between sequences of events or elements of your story.

—beverlyboy.com/filmmaking

Our first Atlanta area house was in the valley of a new development *off* Chamblee Tucker Road. Yvette and Burt moved to a house *on* Chamblee Tucker Road, a terribly busy highway.

One afternoon Dad was coming home early and was highly annoyed by the negligence of the parents of a little boy he witnessed traveling on a tricycle alongside the hazardous road. *The stupidity of these parents! Where were his parents? How could anyone allow their child on the highway?* Someone needed to get this child out of harm's way! He slowed down. Recognized the boy. It was Clark. Dad stopped and promptly put his son and trike in the car and drove home to find the entire household napping, none the wiser to the escape artist.

How did Clark get up the hill? What would make him seek a dangerous adventure? Who was he going to see? Why didn't he take a sibling along? Was he going to see Bobby and turned left instead of right? The answers to these questions were less important than how could my Mother let this happen!

We lived on Cravat Court. Sounds ritzy. It was a nice area. We had a three-bedroom, two-story house with a carport entrance into our den and kitchen. Seasonal photos were taken at the front door, and we occasionally opened it for a Fuller Brush® or encyclopedia salesman. The den was where we congregated. The living room held Mom's starter library with one full bookcase where the parents might hold court if adult guests were present. There were three bedrooms upstairs. The boys had their own room. My room was technically the guest bedroom, depending on who was in town. I room hopped. Most of my toys were in the boys' room, where we all played half the time, but as a rule, I was the odd man.

Our bedtime routine was to take a bath, brush our teeth, and use the toilet. We were to avoid wetting *any* bed, per Mom. Each of us did at some point. Never a fun moment. I don't recall our parents ever buying mattress covers. We'd just flip the mattress when it happened, and the next day flip it again, scrub, and air it out. Bedwetting back then was a hush-hush subject. It was the equivalent of becoming a future Peter Lorre in Fritz Lang's German thriller *M. M* was a black-and-white movie about a serial killer of children. Peter Lorre was Hans Beckert, hunted by the police as children would go missing. Not that I saw *M* as a child, but I do recall how parents generally made a big deal of not wanting to raise a bed wetter. Magazine slugs and Dr. Joyce Brothers' advice columns attacked fun-loving, bed-wetting children everywhere. Editors fueled adult fears by suggesting a hidden meaning behind their child's behavior. Perhaps, if an article opened with "no drinks before bedtime" and "take more trips to the bathroom" instead of seeking a psychiatrist, there might have been less parental anxiety. So much for good editorial content. With the proliferation of magazine options, these publishers were all vying for story ideas and subscriptions! However, it was a time when children spent their entire day in the sunshine playing hard and sleeping hard. Where were the drooling articles? I could soak a pillowcase if I was tired. There was nothing creepy or Fritz Lang-worthy among us.

The neighborhood kids on Cravat were elementary age. We were preschoolers. A large group of us were enjoying popsicles in Lilly's (my friend who lived across the street) backyard when I was hit on the back of the head with a toy grenade. At first, I didn't know what hit me. I began crying, and then saw the grenade. It could have been a real grenade for all I knew. I just recognized it as a war toy we'd seen in John's Bargain Store. Toys of the day were a mix of balls, yo-yos, board games, and miniature versions of things adults used. Boys had military toys. Girls had homemaker toys. Talk about indoctrination. Anyway, no one said they were sorry. These mean kids just kept sucking their popsicles and watching me cry. I was a crybaby. So, I went home.

This was also the period when President Kennedy was shot. Our den's black and white television ran continuous *Special Report(s)* and images that didn't mean anything to small children. We knew that whatever this was, it was causing Mom to cry like we'd never seen before. She would stretch the kitchen wall phone cord as far as she could when she wanted to check on us and look at the television. She and Yvette were on the phone for hours! Nothing would console her. It was clearly worse than getting hit in the head with a toy grenade.

During this time, Dad planned to take us on a Florida vacation. Grandma Everly, my paternal Grandmother, and her mother, my Great Grandma Victoria Foster, named for the Queen of her parents' generation, were to join us. Likely to babysit, but knowing Grandma E, as we called her, she'd expect Mom to babysit us while she spent quality time with her son. She was extremely possessive. He was her only child. When we were packed, in the car, and driving off, a report on the radio mentioned bad storms. The grownups were on high alert. I wondered how the rain in Florida was also in Georgia. *It usually stopped.* We only got a few blocks from the house when adult commotion ensued, and we turned around. Dad had averted an estrogen hurricane.

Regardless, the Grandmas stayed for the whole week. This was the only time I remembered Dad relaxing. Workaholism hadn't been invented then. He just needed a family vacation. Any promotion Dad got meant moving to a bigger house. The next new home was being built in a Stone Mountain subdivision directly behind the forthcoming J.D. Bradford Shopping Center. Bradford's was the anchor store. The shopping center would have everything. It was the closest Mom would be to her favorite neighborhood in Montgomery. Everything was in walking distance, except there was no movie theater.

In the meantime, we moved to the New Peachtree Apartments during the building phase. I started elementary school at this time. I'm guessing kindergarten was optional. None of us went to kindergarten. Franky was in second grade. Mom was now using a cab when friends weren't available to lend a ride.

My first-grade teacher was highly irritated by my crybaby behavior. I didn't like her, and as it turns out, she didn't like me either. One eventful morning, I raised my hand, stood by my desk, and said I didn't feel well. The teacher told me to sit down. I projectile vomited a heavy stream of brown liquid and food chunks between a row of desks, upon which she rolled her eyes and told me to go to the nurse's office. The janitor appeared almost instantly and dispersed sawdust over my chunks and swept them into a bucket. I took a long nap on a cot in the nurse's office as they tried to reach Mom. She ordered a cab ride for me. The nurse took me out when the cab came. My only communication with the cabdriver was him watching me from the rear-view mirror. Neither of us talked. Maybe he thought I would throw up? I'm not sure how much information Mom gave him, but he did recommend I let the wind blow on my face, which I did.

A family by the name of Boone was our lifeline at the apartments. Martha Boone was an experienced dressmaker with her own brood of youngsters. Like Grandma June, Martha sewed most of her children's clothes, even coats. Affordable ready-to-wear garments were slowly taking this additional burden off a woman's chore list, but most diehard seamstresses would hear nothing of store-bought dresses. Since we were a retail family, it was more important that Mom remind other mothers of what was readily available on J.D. Bradford's store racks.

Martha Boone made my first-grade talent competition outfit, an exact tailored replica of *Mary Poppins* navy blue full-length coat, maxi skirt, white blouse, and hat. I was Mary Poppins personified. My stage mothers (Mom bought the fabric and Martha provided the talent) made me a showstopping outfit. We'd seen *Mary Poppins* at Atlanta's Fox Theatre as a family. When the talent competition was announced, I came home and told Mom I wanted to sing a *Mary Poppins* song. I had a portable record player Dad got me for Christmas and the 45 RPM of "A Spoonful of Sugar," sung by Julie Andrews, that I rehearsed with daily. I would be lip-syncing in the talent show. My brothers didn't try out for the competition, but we were all excited. This was my stage debut!

The day of, I was dropped off at school in my outfit, along with Martha's kids and my siblings. I was wearing a real theatrical wardrobe, not some flimsy Halloween costume. Martha went back to get Mom, who was running late. Mom never believed anything started on time. She was always un-fashionably late. Fashionably late meant you missed a few minutes. Mom could miss the whole thing and wonder why everyone didn't wait until she got there. I don't know if I was the first to perform or one of the first, but time stood still. The stage was huge. I was a tiny Mary Poppins. When they called my name, I went out. Stood in front of a microphone stage right.

The field of parents' and children's faces was overwhelming. They were all smiling and thrilled. I was not. I waited for the music to start. I spotted Mom and Martha arriving and waving. I would have waved back if my arms weren't so heavy. The coat was beginning to cook me. From the wings, my teacher urged, "Sing."

Where was the music? I looked to the teacher and then the audience.

"Sing, sing, sing," she whispered.

Slowly I started. "Just a spoonful of sugar …," expecting someone to put a record on. *This was supposed to pretend, not actual singing!* I was so ashamed everyone was listening to me, not Julie Andrews.

When the deed was done, I was escorted to my mom to watch the other performances. After my debut was a third-grade pair, a boy dressed as Dick Van Dyke's

Bert in the red pinstripe jacket, boater hat, and white pants and a girl dressed as a frilly Mary Poppins danced to the recording of "Supercalifragilisticexpialidocious." My mouth dropped! I tugged at my Mother, "Why do they get a record?"

Mom whispered, "Were you supposed to bring a record?"

Some stage Mother she turned out to be.

Mom always assumed everything was taken care of. No matter the situation, she didn't ask questions and never considered what could go wrong. Mom loved to attend performances *when she got there on time*. She reminded me of a younger version of the fairy god-mother in *Cinderella* who sang "Bibbidi-Bobbidi-Boo." Mom was the godmother *before* she could cast spells with a wand. Mom's inner child trusted teachers and school officials. I was suspicious of the entire system.

If Martha Boone had known I didn't have the music, she would have brought the record! However, all was not lost. The outfit won a third-place yellow rib-bon. Not bad. It couldn't have been my performance.

It was at the New Peachtree Apartments that I became a couch squatter. Meaning when Dad was home, I slept on the couch. I felt like a mini adult. I had my own place with a television and a kitchen. No one else did. My brothers had their own room. They were growing taller and slapping each other with regularity. I'd often jump in the middle to break them up and get a slap intended for the other brother. They never fought me. My attempts at peacemaking earned me plenty of handprints and scratches. Mom would tell them to stop. Then Clark would ball himself on the floor and let Franky finish pummeling him. Once Franky was exhausted, they'd move on to playing.

People who lived at the apartment complex were a mixed bag, passing through. At some point they'd all move, it was assumed. There was a lovely Jackie Kennedy-type married to a rough-looking, hot rod-driving brute. She was expected to raise his kids. It was rumored that he had hit her. She frequently dove off the complex's diving board at eight months pregnant. Mom and Martha whispered that she was determined to lose her baby. She did.

There were also live teenage make-out sessions (when her parents weren't home) of a girl who lived closer to the pool. Any kid who bothered could watch them. She left her curtains open. I stood to gander once, but nothing was of interest to me. I went home.

Speaking of the pool, I hated that pool! We all learned to doggie paddle by being thrown in. Sadistic parental torture, Dad's only way of knowing his children wouldn't drown if unsupervised. Mom wasn't a swimmer. One day he took all three of us to the pool for an afternoon of terror. We couldn't leave the pool until he witnessed us not drowning. I clung tightly to the chain link fence, hoping to avoid the hurling. Dad would pull me by the waist. I'd cling tighter and cry. He'd tickle me. Instant release. Then I was airborne, laughing and crying. To be totally transparent, I had the option to just jump in.

Nope.

When I hit the water, my fingers hurt so badly that I wanted to drown. I popped up, coughing, arms and legs flaying, and paddling. I doggie paddled over to the steps, and then out, I ran. Well, I walked superfast to get away because there was a no-running policy at the pool. Again I clung to the chain link, believing this time would be different. Once was not enough. He tested us over and over. At some point, smarty-pants Franky held his nose and jumped off the diving board to show off. I wished I could hold my nose, but I couldn't feel my fingers. Clark just suffered through the human missile toss, coughing up all the water he'd ingested and returned to Dad like a reluctant boomerang.

Most of our apartment activity centered around the pool's clubhouse. We were expected to stay outdoors and not enter strangers' apartments, since apartments were full of drifters right out of *Route 66*. Martha's was the only apartment we were allowed in—with Mom. And since we'd seen the Beatles on *Ed Sullivan* (I had a mad crush on the cute Beatle, Paul McCartney) we took my record player and Beatles album to the pool's clubhouse to hold a concert for no one. The boys pretended to be the band. I was their go-go girl. Go-go girls danced in fancy cages on television, so we determined the brick grill could be a cage or stage.

When we bored of concert performances, we'd chase each other. The clubhouse's sliding glass doors were always left open so apartment dwellers from the north or south units could access the washers and dryers. We'd run through the doors circling around and around, trying to catch one another. I'm not sure how many rotations we'd made when I hit an invisible force that smashed my nose, smacked my forehead hard, and sent me flying backward onto the concrete sidewalk. The wind was knocked out of me. I couldn't breathe. I couldn't cry. Huffing and puffing, I was too confused to understand that one of the boys had closed the sliding glass door behind him. I had crashed into the door at full speed, resulting in my nose and right wrist being cut and the glass door cracked.

I don't remember how I got home or Mom's reaction. I remember my dad taking me to the pediatrician's office after hours (thankfully, it happened late on a Friday afternoon when he was home). It was just Dad and me. The doctor said my nose would heal, but my wrist needed stitches. Dad looked concerned but teased me to distraction. It was funny and annoying. I was more afraid of the needle that would numb my wrist than the one that would sew me up. I'm not sure if the parents were required to pay for the sliding door. There wasn't any scolding, but mostly relief that things were not worse. Still, there was no celebrity to being the girl who broke the door. If anything, we were the infuriating brats who shut things down at the clubhouse for a day.

We had a local celebrity at the pool once, Atlanta's TV meteorologist Johnny Beckman. I don't know if he was visiting someone or trapped for a stretch in apartment drudgery. I spotted him, and I said to my brothers, "Let's talk to him."

They made sure I did. They grabbed me and pushed me all the way up the fence so I could. The weatherman was inside the chain link, and I was on the outside.

Not one to be shown up by my brothers, I said, "I know who you are. You're Johnny Beckman."

He smiled at me. I hadn't prepared a follow-up. My brothers were satisfied and left. I lingered for a moment then waved goodbye.

If truth be told, Bestoink Dooley was Atlanta's real celebrity! At least to us. He was the 11:30 pm host of the Friday night horror show *The Big Movie Shocker*. We were allowed to stay up on Fridays and watch Bestoink introduce scary movies and do some silly antics. He wore a bowler hat and a suit. To me, he looked like a clown who couldn't afford makeup. The show featured

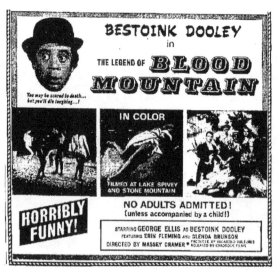

mostly classic horror like *Frankenstein, The Mummy, Dracula,* and *Creature from the Black Lagoon.* Really scary stuff! We were afraid of the dark because monsters are real. *Why else would there be so many monster movies?* We trusted Mom to guard our locked doors.

Mom liked Boris Karloff and Bela Lugosi best. We'd play variations of Dracula, Frankenstein, and the Mummy, fiends with very distinct moves. A cape to the face, arms outstretched, or sluggish leg. Since we didn't have many props, the occasional white candy cigarette sticks with a red flame tip worked well. The rest was up to our imagination. Every horror film had a distracted smoker or clueless victim who never looked over his or her shoulder until the ghoul was right on top of them. Then BAM! Gotcha. And those cigarettes were tasty, too!

Family movie-going shifted from dressing up to attend the Fox Theatre new releases to pajama parties at the drive-in movie. That way, Dad could rest, too. The family station wagon was also his work vehicle, a mobile office. We were not allowed to go to the concession stand but were to stay in the car and keep our hands to ourselves. When the parents returned with popcorn and soda, they'd pass it through the wagon's back window to the three of us. This did not always turn out well, and for some reason, they'd replace the spilled items instead of teaching us a lesson. *They wanted to be away from us **that much***. The movies ranged from Disney's *The Swiss Family Robinson* and *101 Dalmatians,* films that interested us, to their favorites *West Side Story, Lawrence of Arabia, How the West Was Won,* and *Goldfinger.*

Gone with the Wind

The most important theme in Gone with the Wind *is subject to the perspective of the reader because the book has so many themes layered in its story. Nonetheless, survival is one of the most prominent themes in* Gone with the Wind *and it is made more vivid by the theme of war in the story. There are also prominent themes of race, gender, and morality in the story.*

—*bookanalysis.com/margaret-mitchell/*
gone-with-the-wind/

I don't know when I first saw *Gone with the Wind* in a movie theater or how many times I saw it. I just felt as my mother did: there was something unexpected about the women in the story. I was too young to understand war then. Slavery wasn't a topic anyone discussed, so I was clueless as to the struggle within the Civil War narrative. The only war our public school covered to my memory was the Revolutionary War, and even that was limited. I remember the pilgrims and Indians farming and sharing Thanksgiving. That's about it. What I did learn about Abraham Lincoln in my elementary years was minimal. However, what stands out about *Gone with the Wind* was not war or why the war was being fought, but the women who were abandoned for men's fascination with guts and glory. The men rushed out with a fool's confidence that they could take their adversary down in a month or so and be victorious. The cause, though alluded to, was never really defined. This seemed realistic, given the male characters really didn't seem to care what they were fighting for, so long as they were fighting.

However, the women (with one major exception, Melanie) were less enthusiastic about their men running off. Most of the feminine characters ran makeshift hospitals, fed friend and foe, at times were jealous of one another, fought off marauders, provided for and managed their elders, servants, and children—whether their men lived or died. That was my childhood perspective.

From the start of the film we see spoiled Scarlett, her Irish Catholic parents, business manager mother Ellen, flighty father Gerald, her jealous sisters, her Mammy, her crush Ashley and his cousin soon-to-be bride Melanie, and the scallywag Captain Rhett Butler. Everyone had their place around Scarlett. I didn't know what a Mammy was then. I thought she was a nanny or a maid like *Hazel.* I loved her grandmotherly admonishment of Scarlett. However, had I known about slavery then, it would have possibly been confusing. How would Mammy be allowed to raise and reprimand children, while also being reprimanded and owned herself? I would have understood slavery was wrong.

I loved Mammy, Prissy, Pork, and Big Sam for helping Scarlett (whether by choice or circumstance—I was clueless). These characters were endearing. The white trash Scarlett's mother Miss Ellen had to deal with (according to Mammy) stuck in my head. It felt oddly relatable, even to my elementary brain. I remember telling Mom how much I liked Mammy. She said she did, too. Then she told me Hattie McDaniel, who had played Mammy, had won an Academy Award for her performance, and that David O. Selznick had been smart to tell the story of the South in a way that was safer than D.W. Griffth did in his first film. This went right over my head. I didn't ask. Being movie connoisseurs, we were used to talking about actors, directors, and watching the Oscars that were telecast from the Dorothy Chandler Pavilion in Los Angeles. I trusted Mom knew what she was talking about.

Deep in my subconscious, I felt I would be a disappointment to Mammy. I wanted her approval. I loved her as a mother figure. These complicated women consumed me. Prissy and Aunt Pitty-Pat were younger and older versions of naïve, delightful, and fearful women with and without privilege. Belle, the gorgeously scandalous lady-of-the-evening with the means to be charitable to a community too pious to accept, represented honesty. Melanie, on the other hand, was deemed a role model for her overt kindness and understanding of Scarlett's impetuous nature. I didn't trust her. Her own husband, Ashley, didn't like war, but obliged himself to participate. When her brother Charles died, the first casualty, the waif seemed to swell with pride? And why was she so all knowing the night Frank Kennedy died? That woman was on my radar. Still, it was the man-stealing, fashion-conscious, spoiled brat, momma's girl, opportunist, mill owner, reluctant nurse, half-starved, dangerous, Scarlett I banked on. She was flawed, but authentic. How could you not be captivated by these women?

The men were secondary to the women. While Rhett was a handsome devil, he was no match for Scarlett and even says so. Intriguing and impossible to look away from, Rhett's screentime without Scarlett is marginal. We needed them together. While Ashley was vainly embarrassed by her, he too was nothing without her scene-wise. We're supposed to believe Ashley is modest, but like his wife, Melanie, he's dishonest and reveals early on how Scarlett stirs him. Melanie is dependent on Scarlett, and will follow her lead to stay safe, but make no mistake about it, Melanie is cause-focused to a fault. She's the most complicated character of the cast. We're supposed to believe she's a weakling with the book-learning that elevates her above Scarlett, but she feels like a fraud, and an opportunist. If it weren't for her health, she'd be on the battlefield.

Part One closes with Scarlett scavenging a few radishes and declaring, "As God is my witness, I shall never go hungry again."

My mother whispered, "You're like Scarlett." What an odd thing to say to a little girl. Mom planted a radish seed in my thoughts.

As the film comes back from intermission, Scarlett eventually marries Rhett. I was completely confused by the scene where he carries her kicking and screaming up the stairs and then the next morning she wakes smiling and happy. I asked my mom why Scarlett was happy?!

She said, "You know." I didn't. My Rhett-Butler-smitten Mom seemed totally okay with whatever was going on. I was suspicious.

Rhett Butler's "Frankly my dear, I don't give a damn" at the end didn't sit well with me. I wasn't supposed to cuss. Was this necessary? But I knew Scarlett would bounce back. She'd raise Melanie's baby and console dear old Ashley, but not marry him after Mellie died. He was no longer someone else's and besides, he didn't have a head for business. How was that going to work?

I worried for a long time if Rhett would ever return. I battled that thought in my head, and concluded he would. He'd likely end up a guest on her new Mississippi riverboat *La mère de Bonnie* (Bonnie's mother) and rekindle the flame. Well, that's how I'd start a sequel.

The overarching theme was the same as *The Wizard of Oz*. There's no place like home.

Tara would always be Scarlett's first love, since the movie opened on the porch of her childhood home and closed at the foggy doorway of the home where she's lost her child and Rhett. As long as Scarlett had a place to call home, she would survive. My mom also shared that when I authored her story someday, she would like the title to be *The Red Clay Hills of Georgia.*

Write!?

I could barely read. How was I to grow up to be *both* the irritatingly bold Scarlet and her author Margaret Mitchell? Totally unrealistic.

Box Office

Defined as: an office (as in a theater) where tickets of admission are sold.

—*merriam-webster.com*

When our new house was finally built and the official moving day had arrived, the whole city of Atlanta came to a standstill. It was literally *The Day the Earth Stood Still.* Traffic didn't move. Our movers could not get our furniture to the new house because the Beatles were jamming up the interstates and local roads. This was fine by me. I was twisting (and shouting on the inside) looking for Paul McCartney, my future husband. *So, this is how we would meet.* He'd wave to me from a nearby vehicle. I'd wave back. He'd wait for me to grow up and then ask for my hand in marriage. Since our great-grandmother Foster had traveled from Liverpool to America in about 1906, the only thing I had to worry about is …*if Paul and I were somehow related.* Oh, that's just silly. Anyway, Mom was right about answered prayer!! I kept my eyes peeled.

Dad was not happy with the Fab Four. Not only did the mop-top boys hold the city in gridlock, but they also caused a shortage of motel rooms. After an exhausting day in traffic, we eventually found a motel room in another town. If you asked my Dad about that day, he would tell you it was The Beatles' fault!

Our new house was within walking distance of Stone Mountain Plaza's new J.D. Bradfords store, among other competitors. The Stone Mountain area is home to what looks like a moon that crashed on earth. This ginormous rock was also being carved with what would be the image of three Civil War generals riding on horseback. Very sci-fi. When we lived there, we'd take Sunday drives to see the progress being made. It was our first exposure to art and sculpture. Dad was taken by the craftsmanship and told us it was extremely dangerous work and would take years to complete. On these Sundays, Dad and Mom would discuss their latest read from the home library's collection, *Abraham Lincoln: The War Years* by Carl Sandburg. While they chatted, we kids looked for Cary Grant, who might be hanging off a general's nose. We'd seen the Mt. Rushmore scene in Alfred Hitchcock's *North by Northwest* and surmised that a top box office star would practice similar stunts in Georgia. We also speculated that a cyclops lived at the top of the mountain and lobbed boulders at night out of boredom.

Our new house was on Seaman Circle. Mom said it was a horrible sounding street name chosen by terribly childish men and she demanded they not buy a lot on that street, but Dad ignored her. She would much rather we live on Rear Admiral Street, Commander Place, or Chief Warrant Drive. There was a Seaman Lane, too. Whenever she called a repairman, you could hear her annoyance, loudly spelling out, S-E-A-M-A-N. I just didn't understand what the big deal was. She liked the story *Moby Dick*. Wouldn't author Herman Melville like our neighborhood?

With growing children came new pressures for Mom. It was a good thing security video hadn't been invented then because we would have been caught chasing each other through the J.D. Bradford's lamp department. Whenever Mom heard a crash while shopping, she'd drop everything, find us, and escort everyone out of the store. Interrogations were held at another retailer in the strip center, far from Bradford employee ears. Dad never suffered embarrassment. Mom would have gladly paid any replacement costs if she could, but the shame it would bring a company man was too great. Instead, she reminded us that God was watching, and that we'd need to tell the priest at our next Confession. So, we changed tactics and walked fast with our arms beside us, when trying to catch a sibling.

At about this time, Julie Andrews became a prominent fixture in our film repertoire. We loved her in *Mary Poppins* and even more as Catholic postulant/nun apprentice Maria von Trapp in *The Sound of Music*.

Our parents were very much like Maria and Captain von Trapp. Mom didn't sing but was fun, not worried about housekeeping, and super Catholic, much like Maria. Dad not only looked like Christopher Plummer but was a whistle shy of being the exact same disciplinarian of our Knight household. We, the cast of rowdy von Trapp children scrambled to attention when our captain was home from travel.

Then came Julie Andrews as Jerusha Bromley in *Hawaii.* I only remember one moment. We were late getting in and had to sit in the front row of the theater. It was a packed house. The scene was larger than life. The Hawaiians were going to drown a baby in the sea because it had a birthmark or something wrong. My eyes got big. The baby was crying. Who was going to stop them? *No one!* "The baby," I cried. Aloud. VERY Loud. I became hysterical. People were shushing me.

Mom whispered, "It's a movie. It's not real." But *The Sound of Music* was based on real people! How is this not real? Why were we watching this?

Later came *Dr. Zhivago,* a perplexing love story where the names Lara and Tonya stuck in my head. Julie Andrews wasn't in this one. It was a different Julie, Julie Christie. As junior movie buffs, we now identified actors and actresses we read about in Mom's magazines wherever they appeared. It was all very exciting. Omar Sharif, Dr. Zhivago, was also in *Lawrence of Arabia!* What story or scandal would he be involved in?

Mom would eventually find us magazines of interest to us. Franky bought *Famous Monsters From Filmland.* I read *Tiger Beat.* Clark liked *National Geographic.*

Box Office

As a mid-1960s preteen girl, I was becoming aware of a lot of inconsistencies in how girls and boys were raised. *I was a thinker.* I was to help Mom. The boys didn't help Dad. I wore dresses, the boys wore pants. If I wore pants or pedal pushers, mine had a zipper in the back or stylishly up the side. Boys had zippers in the middle of their pants, which I found unfashionable. I had not seen my brothers' privates. Unless it was during a bath as a baby? The memory was erased. But I noted that the boys could go without a shirt. I could not. If something didn't make sense, I tried to figure it out rather than ask. It all had to make sense. I did not accept explanations that were not thoroughly qualified with accompanying evidence or a complete storyline. "Because I said so" was a red flag! Adult shortcuts in information always prompted a "Why?" How were there no adult rules?

We were to ask permission if we wanted to bring a neighbor kid into the house. Kids couldn't just come in. It was a neighborhood thing. Kids stood outside. The front door required clearance. Until granted, you waited. You might ask if someone could come out to play, but you didn't ask if you could come in. If a kid asked why they couldn't come in, you knew they were a real outsider. It was the motherhood code in our nautical-themed community. Every child was to be visible when a mother looked out her window. If she didn't see who she expected to see, she'd open the front door and call out their name. We'd often listen, then disrupt our playtime to tell a kid their mother was calling for them.

I played with two girls, Susie and Marie. They were on opposite ends of the street. Their families were quite different. Susie's were hillbilly; redneck wasn't a term I knew back then. Marie's were more like mine; her father was a professional, and her mother was a stay-at-home mom. Marie's mother had permanent dark circles under her eyes. My mother's complexion was flawless. Marie's mother was genuinely nice and invited me to dinner a few times. I had permission to eat there.

Susie's mother took off her shirt when she got home from work. She cooked dinner in her shorts, bra, and spatula. Hers was a white cotton torpedo cup bra. If there were fancy bras back then, hers was utilitarian.

My mother's, on the other hand, were a mystery. She always turned herself away from me when she was changing. She was very shielding. I would only know her as fully clothed and stylish. We talked to her outside of a locked bathroom door. So, I didn't see anyone's privates, not Mom's, Dad's, or my brothers'. I'm pretty sure the terms penis and vagina hadn't been invented then. I didn't know these words, much less their definition.

I did meet an older girl who wandered into our neighborhood once and said she was on her period. She mentioned bleeding. I didn't have a clue what she meant. I told my Mother, and she brushed it off like it was an isolated incident. Mom was right. The girl never came back. Isolated incident.

Susie's dad drank Schlitz. My dad didn't drink alcohol that I knew of, well, not in front of us or in

the house to my knowledge. Susie's dad watched television from his recliner when he got home from work,
nursing a can of beer. I wasn't allowed in Susie's house,
but she said it was okay to come in, so I followed her.
Big mistake! Susie had older siblings, of which my
only encounter was her older brother who tied both of
us up in their basement for his own amusement. We
screamed for hours it seemed. At some point, about
dinner time, we were released. I didn't tell my mother.
Instead, Susie and I decided to meet at the blackberry
bushes between our houses to hide from her brother.

Kid communication was the same as mom communication. We called out for one another or looked
for each other in familiar play areas. Telephones were
important communication tools for adults, teachers,
businesspeople, and distant family. You were *not* to call
your friend's house. Even if your mom wanted to call
your friend's house, they would often have to look the
number up in the white pages of the telephone book
by last name. If she didn't know her neighbor's first
name, then last name and address would provide the
desired results, and often the listing was in the father's
not the mother's name. Mom was Mrs. Frank Knight.
Women's first names were for formal introduction and
were often unknown. As for phone numbers in general,
an unlisted number, a second phone, or an additional
phone line cost a lot more.

Dad had an illegal telephone in the spare room at
the Seaman Circle house. Home offices hadn't been
invented then, so technically this was a multi-purpose

room. The spare room was upstairs, the last room on the right across from the parents' bedroom. It had a desk, desk chair, an unloaded rifle mounted on the wall, and Mom's Singer sewing machine in a corner. We kids were not allowed in the spare room but were brought in by Dad and shown a heavy black phone that he locked in one of the desk's drawers. We *weren't* to know about it because it was unlawful to hook up your own phone. I guess if Southern Bell found out, Dad could go to jail. This was technically an underground phone. Dad was worried his family might be an accessory to a crime he'd committed so at least we'd know what not to know. I'm still a little foggy about that.

The house was a split level, which meant the front door was neither on the second nor first floor, but in the middle. The first floor was where the boy's room, the laundry room, the eat-in den, and the garage were. The second floor was Mom and Dad's bedroom, their bathroom, the spare room, my bedroom, and the living room. We didn't use the living room except for Christmas and when a family member visited. Most of the homes on our block had their kitchen where my bedroom was and a dining room where our living room was. Mom had longed to be an interior decorator, so this design change was her inspiration.

Christmas sidebar: Dad loved a tinsel tree, with a color wheel of red, yellow, green, and blue plastic shields rotating in front of a hot lamp. He was equally passionate about glass-blown ornaments of gold, red, blue, and green interspersed in an orderly fashion on the tree's glitzy silver branches. We, Mom included, tolerated Dad's preference. He was proud of the savings the tree represented. He would never have to buy another tree or ornament *ever* again.

My bedroom had a half bath, a walk-in closet, full-sized bed, a side table, an off-white princess vanity, and sitting bench. The vanity had a lid that opened to a mirror that could be locked in place with plenty of storage in the center and two drawers on either side. Mom got me a brush set to keep in the center compartment. I had a pixie cut then, so there wasn't a lot of hair to brush.

As the middle sister between two brothers, I didn't like my room a whole lot. It was too fancy and far away from the action. My room's closet was like a whole other bedroom. I thought my brothers had the better room. It had twin beds, a long desk they could share, two chairs, bookshelves mounted above the desk, and a black and white television. Dad even drilled holes into the shelves for the rabbit ear antenna. *But a television!*

Mom watched the family television downstairs in the den. The boys could easily sneak out and watch if they were clever, but they had their own television. The parents' logic was my spacious room was equal to the boys' slightly smaller room with a television. I was too scared to come down once tucked in and the lights off. If I had to go to the bathroom, I'd go quickly and make a flying leap onto my bed to avoid the monsters hiding underneath. I just knew my ankles were not safe when the lights were off. I'd lay in that big bed wondering what everyone was doing. I never thought to leave the lamp on. Missed opportunities. When Mom came up after her shows (when television stations signed off at midnight with the national anthem and color bars or an Indian-head test pattern), I was asleep.

We went to Dogwood Elementary School just a few blocks up the street. It was ideal for Mom. She only had to wake us, feed us, and lay out our J.D. Bradford wardrobe of school clothes, which consisted of about three outfits that were washed and rotated throughout the school week. School shopping was always limited. We were on a tight budget, and Mom chided Dad that it was not a great representation of the company. He could afford a few more items. Our school clothes, along with Christmas and Easter outfits, made up our wardrobe. The school district did not permit girls to wear pants. Girls wore dresses and skirts. Pants were only allowed under dresses on winter days. I had a pair of girl's corduroy pants for winter. They looked terrible. All the girls looked dumb on snow days: hats, mittens, jackets, dresses, and pants. It felt good but looked awful.

My neighbors Susie and Marie were not in my class. I had five friends in Dogwood Elementary. I can't remember anyone else. They were two negro girls Teresa and Porsha and two negro boys Timmy and Maurice, and one Caucasian girl with braces on her legs, Leslie. Negro was the term used for colored people. White people were called Caucasian. I always thought Caucasian sounded like a caveman term. Black was not a term I'd heard at that time.

Timmy was chubby and funny. He and I often got into trouble for giggling. He sat behind me and braided what short hair I had. We were instructed to pay attention, Timmy to leave my hair alone. Maurice was always well-dressed and very shy. One eventful class Christmas party, he drew my name for the gift exchange. We were not to tell whose name we drew. Gifts were to remain anonymous. That was to protect anyone from the embarrassment of a crappy gift like a Bugs Bunny bubble bath or God forbid your Mom wrapped an unwanted soap-on-a-rope. The giftee would receive their gift at their grade's Christmas party. Maurice got me an orange plastic Tootsie Roll® dispenser/bank. He picked it out himself! He told me.

I was smitten.

Not only was Maurice polite and quiet, but he was also a great shopper. I don't know whose name I drew or what I gave, but I've never forgotten this gift.

Teresa and I were suspicious types. Not of each other, but of the whole playground system. Teresa was short, and Porsha about my height. We were playground mates who didn't play as much as watch the other kids play. Our teachers would always encourage us to get out there with the other girls. We were not impressed. We'd much rather play with the boys. As a tomboy, I didn't understand why the school wanted the girls and boys in separate groups.

Leslie was taller, with short, curly blonde hair and a big, dimpled smile. She was pale and tried her best to run, but her braces would oftentimes lock up, and she'd almost fall over. She was way more ambitious than most of her more physically capable peers.

Leslie and I liked to eat lunch together. We'd often save each other a seat. Lunches were either brought from home or purchased. School cafeteria food was mostly undesirably hot, nutritious food. Milk was available in glass bottles with foil or paper tops that you'd punch your straw through. There was juice, too.

My mom gave us change to buy lunch when she was out of ideas as to what to pack in our metal lunch boxes. School shopping included a new lunch box with our supplies. Supplies took money away from school clothes, and that was fine with us kids. We wanted a new lunchbox, notebook, pencils, paper, crayons, and erasers every year. Television characters dominated the lunchbox scene: *Bonanza, The Munsters, Peanuts, The Flintstones,* and more.

One unforgettable lunch, Leslie had gone in and started before me. I had my tray and found her. She had brought her lunch and bought milk. Leslie always had a paper bag. On this day, she was finished, bored, and blowing bubbles into her nearly empty glass milk bottle. The more she blew her straw, the higher the bubble stack grew. It was magical. I was mesmerized. Leslie's milk bottle was full of fluffy white bubbles. I was going to do that, too! Lunch could wait. I stabbed the straw into my milk bottle and immediately blew as hard as I could.

I then entered Einstein's space-time continuum. Like my sliding glass door accident, time ceased to exist. I was having an out-of-body experience. The next thing I remembered, I was sitting in the principal's office with milk dripping from my hair and the office ladies searching through a mountain of clothing drive donations for an outfit for me to change into. They'd called my Mother, but she didn't answer.

From the point of the big blow to the principal's office, I was teleported through a wormhole of darkness to a tunnel exit of frantic adults. *What was everyone upset about?* Questions were lobbed at me: "Why did you do this? Who else is responsible? Did someone dare you?"

I had milk explosion amnesia.

More humiliating, a lunchroom full of peers had witnessed something I could not remember. But worse still, I had to wear another student's mother's oversized dress the rest of the day, and home from school. My Mom couldn't understand why I had on ill-fitting clothing when she had sent me to school in an appropriately sized clean dress. She probed, "What is going on at that school? Why do you smell sour?"

I had questions, too! We had two phones, one downstairs and the illegal one locked upstairs. How did Mom miss the school's call? Was she on the split level when the phone rang and couldn't get downstairs in time? Or was she upstairs and couldn't find Dad's desk key to hook up the illegal phone? Would the call have been traced if she had answered the criminal phone? Would we be orphaned if the call had been traced to the felonious phone? Did the school call more than once? Was I setting my family up for a big fall?

A little Catholic education goes a long way. Was I a little Eve, but instead of an apple, I was tempting my Mother to use *that* phone? Would God understand? Should I confess this?

When I went back to school, no one pointed or laughed. They had moved on. Kids had more important things to concern themselves with than the *milk girl*, thankfully. We were there to learn, play, and socialize.

I can't say I was more than an average student. I loved history homework and drawing maps, especially coloring them in. I was a tracing color-er. This means I liked to trace after vs. outline before coloring a pictured item. Mom was an outliner. She would often color with us. You didn't have to twist her arm. We could all get into a coloring frenzy at the kitchen table and often had an argument over who was bearing down on the crayons and making them less pointy. We each had our own set. The commingled crayons would start a "who done it" mystery that sometimes culminated in hitting, crying, complaining, and favoritism. Mom would divvy up a defective crayon to all of us though she knew who the smasher was. *Didn't she?* At which point we'd all have to go outside and run it off. During these retreat moments, Mom would do laundry, read magazines and books, or think about making dinner.

The laundry room was on the first floor underneath the office. The boys' closet backed up to the laundry room. The laundry room was a portal of clandestine activity. We'd watched *Mission Impossible, I-Spy,* and *The Man from U.N.C.L.E.,* but preferred *Get Smart.* Espionage games required escape routes, keys to hidden places, and at least three kids to make it worth playing. Someone had to be the bad guy. These were Dad's favorite shows, and to our surprise he cut a hole into the drywall of the boys' closet to give us an escape route into the laundry room. A most considerate gesture from Captain von Trapp!

When Dad was home, we weren't to talk during television shows. Remote controls, pause, and rewinding had not been invented then. He had rules. We were not to call Mom, her, or she, but Mom. When we were eating, we were to chew with our mouths closed, go to bed when told, stay in bed, wait our turn, say our prayers, behave, and BE QUIET. He once photographed us to resemble the monkey statues: Hear No Evil, Speak No Evil, and See No Evil.

The laundry room and the boys' closet were the closest thing we'd ever have to a playhouse. Dad saw to that. However, there was a BIG laundry room scandal that almost marred our love for that room. It was a Sunday evening. Mom was readying Dad's laundry for travel. Dad peeked his head in to say something to Mom and witnessed vandalism on the wall, up high, near the washer. *Was Mom blind?* Who did it? Which child?

Dad called a family meeting. The three of us stood at attention before our parents. Dad asked us if we knew why we had been called into the laundry room.

The three of us looked at each other and around the room. We shrugged. Dad then pointed to the wall.

A very smart-looking secret agent-style pistol had been drawn on the wall in brown crayon. Duh! Duh! Duh!

I looked at my older brother, who was a budding artist. He was admiring the artistic quality. We knew Clark couldn't reach that high. Well, nor could we.

Dad said, "Who did this?"

We all muttered something about not drawing a gun on the wall. To which Captain von Trapp snapped and said, "Not the gun, what's written under it." Duh! Duh! Duh!

Dad eyed us all suspiciously, even Mom.

Mom was really a good suspect. She was tall and had access to the crayons. Maybe in a fit of anger she wrote a bad word on the wall and covered it up.

I raised my hand, "Can we draw on the walls?"

Dad gave the *Dracula* stare. *Got it. No.*

The parents never said what the word was that Dad told us not to write again. We all had to go to bed early and think about it. The three of us went to the boys' room and thought about it. We concluded it had to be a cuss word. And the only cuss words we knew were hell, damn, crap and the one that would send you *to hell*, taking the Lord's name in vain. It had to be one of those, but by Dad's reaction, it had to be one we hadn't heard.

Since Dad couldn't determine the vandal, he didn't take out the belt. Dad spanked us with a belt maybe four times ever. We certainly deserved it for offenses he was unaware of, like running in Bradfords. But when he determined we'd crossed a behavioral line that needed correction, he'd have all three of us sent in one by one for our individual punishment. Clark and I cried as the belt was in the air. Loudly. One or two whacks and we were done. Franky was the brave one. He tried not to cry and got more whacks. Clark and I would listen. Dad didn't want to punish Franky more, but Dad needed him to react. We tried to tell Franky, but bravery was his thing. *No thanks!*

Speaking of getting into trouble, Mom got herself in hot water with Dad when she convinced him to take the whole family to see the movie *Georgy Girl* at the theater. Dad trusted her. He didn't look in the newspaper to see the movie listing or posters. *Georgy Girl* was about a young London woman having relations with boyfriends outside of marriage. Not appropriate viewing for children, especially Catholic children. Mom had overlooked these points as she was intrigued by a new release. Dad got our tickets. The movie had already started. It was dark, and we all moved into a row of seats. He barely sat when he saw Lynn Redgrave making out and rolling around with a man on the screen. Up he stood and marched us all out. Game over. Mom lingered a moment longer, holding up the rear. She wasn't going to see this movie ever, so she may as well have a look. Dad got a full refund, and we went home.

We were to have clean minds and clean hearts. And we were a fairly healthy bunch. Everyone got the polio vaccine in the 1960s. When I say we, I mean Mom and us kids, since we were a potential house of contagion if one of us got something. Dad had received his shots in the military and whenever. We knew nothing of his doctor's visits. Some of us got measles, chicken pox, and the mumps. The MMR (Measles, Mumps, and Rubella) vaccine hadn't been invented then. If you had a fever, you chewed Bayer® Aspirin for Children. Mom used Absorbine Jr. on cuts and scrapes. Its packaging said it was meant for sore muscles, arthritis, and hot, itchy feet. I'm not exactly sure how that translated to cuts and scrapes, but that's what she used. It came in a glass bottle with green liquid and a Pres-O-Matic applicator.

We were told if ever stepped on a rusty nail, we'd have to get a tetanus shot. I feared shots. We weren't a careful bunch when we played Pilgrims and Indians in the creek behind our house. Pilgrims caught crawfish and drank creek water in the New World. So did we. As luck would *not* have it, I punctured one of my shoes with a nail. The nail pierced my shoe and broke the skin on my foot. I immediately began top-secret Absorbine Jr. treatments, telling no one. The boys were rat finks. I didn't want a shot. My wound didn't bleed, but my shoe did leak if I stepped in a puddle. So, I had to be cautious. As it turns out, I survived.

Mom had a short bout with illness around late 1967 that sent us all packing to North Carolina. I remember a church lady picked us all up after school one afternoon so that Mom could rest.

Adults shielded their illness and injury from children in those days. I remember Dad did some yardwork on a Saturday and came into the house looking gray. Mom told us all to be quiet and go outside while she tended to Dad. I'm sure she used Absorbine Jr. on his wound. She later told us once Dad was asleep that he'd nicked his leg with the ax chopping at something. Shh! We weren't supposed to know.

We never knew what her classified top secret mystery illness was either. Dad decided she needed to get some medical attention and us some supervision, so Dad moved us in with Grandma Everly and Great Grandma Foster in Charlotte. This was a place we knew from prior visits, the house where Dad was born. Ancient. We were even enrolled in elementary school in North Carolina, much to our shock and dismay. This was a vacation or Christmas visit destination, not a place for children to *live*.

I had the same elementary teacher as my Dad. How was that possible? Shouldn't the woman be dead? Mrs. Cartwright was about Grandma's age, a fixture at Thomasboro Elementary. The school was within walking distance from Grandma's house. The three of us walked together with a sea of other children from nearby streets.

It was a turbulent time. The Civil Rights Movement was stirring up adults all over the country. Adults segregated themselves and their kids. Martin Luther King, Jr. and Robert Kennedy, Jr. were people I wanted to be like. RFK promoted Peace Corps missionary work to foreign lands and MLK promoted all people getting along in a nonviolent way. They made sense. Nothing else did.

At the same time, gorillas were fighting in Vietnam. I didn't know the word guerilla then, so I was really impressed by the species. I could not see the gorillas that Huntley and Brinkley reported as fighting in the jungles of Vietnam. I saw soldiers with rifles, but never gorillas. So, the complaints about a war that would never end made sense. Those gorillas were an elusive bunch. They would never catch them.

Neither Dad nor Mom ever told us what was wrong with Mom. Women didn't talk about their health. Everything was silenced. I thought Dad and Grandma were up to something. Kids see and attempt to hear everything. Mom was admitted to Compassion Hospital for a week and came out good as new. Time to go home. But Grandma and Dad talked like Mom wasn't well enough to return to Georgia. She needed time to build up her stamina, and what better way than managing three kids and Great Grandmother?

We were trapped.

Dad now drove to Charlotte to see us every few weeks. What began as a short-term plan became a great unknown. We wanted to get back to our Seaman Circle house, but there was no date on the horizon. Thankfully, our cousins lived close by and made the experience less isolating. Sundays we'd all go to Mass with the grandmas, our aunt, and the cousins. Then we'd eat the standard English fare: meat and potatoes (the only meal Great

Grandmother made on Sundays). Pressure-cooked beef roast with sliced potatoes and a whole onion. I'm not complaining. It was always delicious.

The sleeping arrangements at Grandma's were Mom in a twin bed and the boys in a bunk bed all sharing the same room, and me sharing a bed with my namesake grandma. Great Grandma was in her own room unless Dad was in Charlotte. Then he and Mom would sleep together in Great Grandmother's room. Great Grandmother slept with Grandmother in her room, and I slept in the twin bed Mom normally occupied next to the boys' bunkbed.

I felt like Cinderella *before* the glass slipper.

Up to this point, I had never heard anyone snore. Grandma didn't sound human when she was sleeping. She sounded like something from *Mutual of Omaha's Wild Kingdom.* It was so unfair! Not only did I have to listen to that each night, but I was also pinned next to the window. Grandma was a heavy back sleeper and hogged most of the bed. My only solace was watching the activity at the Texaco station a block up the street. Grandma lived off the interstate, and the gas station was always busy. When the station closed, the lone streetlight stayed on. I watched that light every night until the sandman took me from waking nightmare to dreamland.

If I had to go to the bathroom, I crawled to the foot of the bed and wandered through the darkness until I heard the giggling of Mom, Clark, and Franky. Their room was next to the bathroom. Mom really didn't have *enough* sympathy for me. Why couldn't she sleep with Grandma?! She said it would hurt Grandma's feelings if I complained about her snoring or asked to sleep in the den or living room. Since I'd been a couch dweller before, couldn't I do it again? But no, I had to be a good girl and keep the peace. I prayed God was keeping score.

The upside to Grandma's room: she had a radio. While she was at work, I could listen to Gary Puckett and the Union Gap, The Monkees, Simon and Garfunkel, The Beatles, Smokey Robinson, Aretha Franklin, and Marvin Gaye. My record player was at home, so this was my sanctuary. I would sing and dance to my favorites, "Ode to Billie Joe," "Light My Fire," "Daydream Believer," "Georgy Girl," "All You Need Is Love," "Respect," "Beautiful Morning," "Indian Lake," "Love Is All Around," "Lady Willpower," "MacArthur Park," "People Got to Be Free," "Love Child," "Revolution," "Sounds of Silence," "Judy in Disguise," and "Sea Cruise." Grandma didn't listen to the radio

except for the news, and she didn't want it on when she was home. So, I cherished radio time, along with our afternoon routine watching *Dark Shadows*.

Great Grandmother didn't approve of vampires, and thankfully she napped in the afternoon. When she did emerge to our gasps of horror (often without her glasses), she couldn't make out what was on the television. She and Grandma had clear classifications of what made up a devil worshipper. The gateway was black turtlenecks, men with long fingernails, beatnik poetry, rock and roll music, monster movies, midriffs, writing with your left, and hip huggers, to name a few.

I'm left-handed, so Grandma had a discussion with Mom and Dad about converting me to right-handed. Mom is right-handed and taught me how to crochet as we sat side-by-side. I could chain stitch crochet with my right hand. God met me halfway. Grandma dropped the subject.

When Grandma wasn't around, we also bought waxed candy fingertips and vampire teeth at the candy counter of the local drug store. We were moving into the realm of evil by Catholic grandparental standards. Mom loved Barnabas, too. He was quite the dresser and a lady's man. We were *Dark Shadows* groupies.

At 4:30 pm we'd tune into Charlotte's local UNC-TV Clown Carnival with Joey the Clown. On

Fridays he had a weekly segment, Joey's Magic Key, granting a live call to one lucky kid. The kid on the phone would watch the show, pick a key, and we'd all watch to see if the selected key unlocked a fenced-in corral of toys. The phone rang at Grandmother's house at the same time Joey was calling. We all froze. It couldn't be. Could it? We ran to the phone. I can't remember who answered, but it was Grandma on the line. We were sad. A bit mad, too. Joey might be trying to get through! This was before call waiting was invented. Grandma *never* called! Why now? To be honest, I'm sure there was more to Joey's caller selection than a random phonebook pick. But to us, we were *this* close.

Speaking of close, how close have you ever been to a rat, unintentionally? Grandma's house and yard were infested with rodents of varying shapes, sizes, and ages. How do I know? Behind her house was a two-acre unmowed field. There were two small porches attached to the house, one screened in, one unscreened. A large L-shaped trimmed hedge blocked the field from the street view. Just behind the hedge was a rusty swing set on a patch of mowed yard, our play area. Behind the swing set was rat field.

At some point Grandma owned a riding lawn mower. She didn't allow us to mow without supervision. I do remember getting a chance to mow the nicer section of the property by the front of the house. I sang at the top of my lungs while mowing, figuring no one could hear me. Wrong! Dad had started the mower and was listening the whole time, grinning from ear to ear. I wanted to die! It's hard to explain, but Dad was like a special guest when he was home. You wanted his approval, and you didn't want to embarrass yourself.

Back to the rats and mice. One particularly sunny day, I had ventured out to the rusty swing set alone to sing at the top of my lungs, "Yummy Yummy" by Ohio Express. I was standing on the horizontal bar of the A-frame support, belting out a tune, when I decided to hang upside down and continue my solo. At some point I felt I was being watched. A rat or a mouse scurried up to have a look at the upside-down songstress. I swear I saw teeth! I screamed. It ran. Next thing I remember, I was clinging to the top of that tetanus trap, shrieking and shaking! With the highway noise and the distance of the swing set to the house, my cries were completely drowned out. The only way Mom would've heard me is if she were sitting on the side porch or trying to stop Great Grandma from throwing food off the kitchen steps, another problem altogether.

I come from a long line of indoor people. Sure, a grownup would begrudgingly sit and watch one or more of us at a park, but not because it was their preference. To be fair, Mom had a lot more experience outdoors. But Dad was a suit guy. He'd make an appearance at a barbecue wearing suit pants, his white shirt sleeves rolled up, and no tie. That was casual. Mom once challenged Dad and Burt to take all of us kids camping at Lake Lanier without the moms. Challenge accepted. The executive dads wasted a lot of time. We pitched tents by flashlight. I was the only girl in the bunch, so I proudly told my dad I wasn't afraid of a daddy-long-legs bug crawling in our tent—until he threw one on me! Thrashing and screaming, I withheld further contact until the next day's fishing lessons.

On a different combo indoor-outdoor vacation, we stayed at Vogel State Park cabins as a family. Again, we got there late. Knight time. The cabins were pitch black with the lights off. You couldn't see your hand in front of your face, a terrifying thought for monster movie fans. *What else could you not see?*

Anyway, Dad taught us to *not talk* while fishing. Mom stayed inside reading. We had a lakeside cabin with plenty of fresh air and a beautiful view. I was so thrilled to see a big trout swim up to my line that I yelled to Dad. "LOOK!" The fish swam away. *There was something to the not talking thing.* Then Dad left us alone so he could take a nap. Clark decided to swing his cane pole back and show us how the bigtime fishermen cast. Then he snagged his leg and shorts. *Panic!* We became stealthy about not talking. *Did Mom pack Absorbine Jr.?*

Clark was going to need a tetanus shot! Our heightened fear of needles began after receiving polio shots. Needles were bigger then. Nurses and doctors held you down or very tight to get a shot over with. Medicine was a no-nonsense business. We argued over who would work the hook out. I pushed Franky. Franky shoved me. He said it was Clark's own fault. We took turns until we got the hook out. The only blood drawn was from our faces when Dad came out later and asked us how we were doing. We didn't understand the sin of omission, so it wasn't lying when we said, "Fine." And Clark lived.

Back to the rats of Charlotte. The kitchen entrance was up a set of stairs at the back of the house. Great Grandma threw old food, grease, and things she didn't want in the garbage can over the rail for (she believed) cats who needed fuel to kill the rats. It was really the rats that feasted on the food she dumped, and a cat might join in, but there were not enough cats to battle the rodent population.

At dusk one grocery shopping day, I paused in the ankle-deep grass at the kitchen steps to listen to Mom tell me to watch where I was going as something gray brushed by my foot. It was an old rat I assumed. I figured they were as old as my grandmother since they had the same hair color. I was becoming adept at screaming and running. Up the stairs I went.

Mom tried to convince Great Grandmother to stop throwing food into the yard. But the old Brit would hear nothing of it. By English standards these were field mice. We didn't know a thing about rats! She continued throwing scraps.

Another time, I trust Dad was lying to me, but I took it to heart. He witnessed my leg dangling off the twin bed and a mouse standing on its hind legs sniffing my toes. The horror! He made it sound like a *Stuart Little* adventure. Where was God?

Speaking of God, we went to Mass at St. Peter's Catholic Church in downtown Charlotte on Sundays.

We were even enrolled in Sunday school class there and attended! Grandma ran a tight God-fearing ship! Grandma and Aunt Agnes (her sister) were members of St. Peter's Altar Society. I was invited to join in on their Saturday duties.

St. Peter's saint statues had beautifully painted eyes that followed you. I was awe struck by Jesus-the-statue. He watched my every move as I dusted the altar. But the real shocker of church duties was filling the holy water container from the church's sink! How was this not blasphemy? Didn't they truck in holy water from Jerusalem or something? Turns out, no. You fill the tank with tap water. The priest blesses it. Presto, holy water! The mysteries of faith were no longer so mysterious.

I was to observe. Be silent and reverent. No talking. Occasional whispers permitted. And P.S. Grandma hogged all the flower duties. I caught Aunt Agnes rolling her eyes at her sister.

When it came to Mass on Sunday, Great Grandmother insisted I walk her down the aisle to communion. Since I had made my First Communion, we'd both be receiving communion together.

Funny thing, I actually listened to the Mass while at St. Peter's. Father Ed had a fire and brimstone approach. He would nearly lull you to sleep and then slam his fist on the pulpit to make a point. The microphone would squeal. His voice would boom. I'd glance at Jesus-the-statue. He'd look at me with that 'love thy neighbor' expression. The whole Altar Society thing changed me.

I soon began to dread the Eucharistic Prayer. Thinking about the body and blood of Christ made me lightheaded. I would imagine sweet Jesus-the-statue all bloody and being held by Mary after he'd been taken off the cross. Butchered for communion. I was ready to pass out when Great Grandma would nudge me to take her up the aisle. What she didn't know was she walked *me* to communion. How was receiving the Body of Christ normal? I continued to go through the same wooziness each week. Like please, God, *not again!*

My Dad walked me outside once when I went pale. He sat me on the church steps. He told me to look at my shoes. "Put your head between your legs to get the blood flowing."

When he asked me what was wrong, I whispered, "The body and blood."

He told me I was taking it all too seriously. But I wasn't. Adults were always emphasizing to behave, listen carefully and understand God was watching our every move. And God sent his son Jesus to *die* for us because everyone had been naughty and not nice. Right? Was God really Santa Claus?

Dad truly didn't get it. He thought he could get away with stalling, driving slowly to church, and skipping out. But what he didn't know was God was counting on me to save our family. Of this I was certain. I was the vocation the church was grooming for the nunnery. Dad needed to watch more televangelists with Grandma June. Or more *Life Is Worth Living with Bishop Fulton J. Sheen* which we watched with Mom.

You'd think I'd want to avoid Mass because of my communion syndrome. Not so. I was on a mission. The grandmothers and Aunt Agnes were my people. We were church ladies, an elite club. Church insiders. Now when I vacuumed the altar carpet it was me and Jesus spending time together. He could watch all he wanted!

Grandma drove us to church in her blue and white Chevy with fins, the closest thing to a Batmobile if it had been painted black. It seemed enormous. Seatbelt laws were just beginning then, but her car didn't have any. We slid when she turned. During midweek Kentucky Fried Chicken runs, we had specific orders to hold that bucket tight. Grandma always let us kids fight over who would hold the bucket, instead of giving the duty to her daughter-in-law in the front seat. It was a control thing. Franky was the number one bucket holder. If the lid popped, no one was safe. Grandma would scream and grab for us while driving. We were all hostages of the runaway Chevy. Mom would look daggers at us and grit her teeth, and mouth things. She was an expert at voicing nothing in tense situations.

Grandma seriously believed that any heat that escaped the KFC˚ lid (which had vent holes!) would ruin the freshness. There was no consoling an early KFC bucket-lid release. She would cry. The boys did pop the lid once and Jesus took the wheel. Only He could save us from the wrath of the fried chicken czaritza and oncoming motorists. It was never fun. The best part was eating. Grandma's heat factor equation required us to get to the table fast for freshness' sake.

Grandma got first dibs at the chicken. Great Grandma had to move faster, as no one waited. She could shuffle for chicken. We said grace in our heads on KFC nights as time was of the essence. Sunday dinner we might say an extended grace and ask for forgiveness for our lust of the 11-Herbs and Spices Original Recipe deep-fried poultry. The medicinal effect of KFC set in when the bucket was empty and our bellies full. Only then were the boys too sluggish to hit each other.

Only Franky could top Grandma's bucket obsession. He was a leg man, loved drumsticks. Had to have them—until he got a vein stuck between his teeth. He wailed. Great Grandma continued to eat and point at Mom. Grandma ate and watched Mom. Mom looked a little concerned. Clark began to laugh. I wanted to pass out thinking about it. *Why would they sell us chicken with veins?* I was no longer sure I could eat chicken… with veins. Mom found a toothpick in the kitchen. Dental floss wasn't a household item then, so it was tough going. Eventually, the vein was dislodged, and Franky restored to his noble older brother status. We were not to tease him.

That summer I turned ten and Mom and Dad took me shopping. Just me. This was a special trip, but for *them*. They looked at me differently. Made me very uncomfortable. We went to a nice department store. It was time I get fitted for a new outfit, shoes, and a training bra. Training bra! Training for what? To be like Elizabeth Taylor? I was aware of bras thanks to Susie's mom and of course Elizabeth Taylor, Sophia Loren,

Jayne Mansfield (who died in a car crash that year), and all the breast-y women on the movie magazine covers. I wanted no part of growing … those. To think my parents were looking at mine was terrifying.

I was noncommittal on Mom's bra selections. I just nodded at anything to get it over with. Then we went to look for pants and a blouse. The pants Mom suggested were fuchsia and made of a heavy knit fabric with ribbed piping and wide flared legs. Fancy! They weren't hip huggers but were very Twiggy. Twiggy wore a lot of bold colors. I loved Twiggy and these pants! I felt I could go *Downtown* like the Petula Clark song.

Next, we picked a white peasant blouse with slightly puffy sleeves. I hated the bra less by this point because I'd never thought about anyone wanting to look at my chest and it was high time to hide these things. *They were right!* Then the parents picked out some black patent leather flats. Not the strappy Mary Jayne kind that I'd worn all my life, but the kind grown women slip on to go to lunch or church. I stepped into the first pair and saw the deep scooped edge around my toes. These shoes showed way more feet than my Mary Jaynes. They were expensive high gloss black flats. The parents were beaming. *I gasped.* Toe cleavage! These flats were showing the divide between my big toe and the toe next to it! Disgusting. I didn't want Elizabeth Taylor feet. What were they thinking? I had tears in my eyes that were mistaken for joy. We bought everything. I was miserable. How had everything about my 10th birthday turned to cleavage?

I fully expected my brothers to have something disgusting to look forward to, too. As far as I could tell, the boys might get a voice change, but they didn't have to wear bras or have babies someday. What else were they not telling me?! As for the subject of babies, I knew nothing, except that women had them when they got married. I wished for a baby sister on each birthday cake. From what television, movies, and even cartoons portrayed, having a baby was equal to death. Here's a brief list of shows with no mother: *Bachelor Father, The Rifleman, Bonanza, My Three Sons, The Andy Griffith Show, Quickdraw McGraw, The Alvin Show, Beverly Hillbillies, Flipper, Thunderbirds, Jonny Quest, Gidget, The Farmer's Daughter, Family Affair,* and *To Kill a Mockingbird.*

It seemed Hollywood cared a lot more about cleavage than the dead mother storyline. Entertainment, it seemed, relied on the death of a mother to give the father freedom to date. That's what I saw. Her death went unavenged. *With so many deadly childbirth storylines, surely the family doctor was a suspect.* But no, he was a welcomed friend and often made exhaustive house calls to all his patients. *So, fate killed her?* It was high time the husband moved on and found a much stronger replacement, a younger, attractive woman who would continue the dead mother's legacy until *she* died from homemaking. Film dads were softies, encouraged to move on and find another wife to care for him and the kids. Stepmom-resistant children would eventually succumb to the other woman's charms, once she discovered their interests. Not me. I got the message loud and clear.

- Don't have babies. They will kill you.
- Don't trust single women. They want to steal your dad—especially if your mom dies.

When our mother was in Compassion Hospital, kids weren't allowed to visit unless they were fourteen, or that's what we were told. We were all under the age of fourteen and Dad and Grandma acted like Mom was still sick even when she got better. People acted like that back then. It was unclear if it was science or bad acting. Women especially, needed long convalescing periods. Not that a woman didn't appreciate a little rest and relaxation, but if a woman felt she was good as new, it was a sign she might be losing touch with reality. Doctors' orders were to be followed. There was no room for common sense. You would not recover in less than the prescribed period. Everyone knew that! His orders were backed by a board of professionals. *There were prescribed medications for questioning authority.*

Mom became suspicious. I was, too. So, she made up her mind to lose weight and play along and work on a plan to get us back to Georgia. At night she did sit ups. During the day she ate cottage cheese, boiled eggs, and apple sauce. She was shedding pounds, buying fewer magazines, and using the savings for bus fare to the movies. Everything was going great until we saw *Planet of the Apes!*

Somehow, Grandma got off early that day. How she figured where we were, I'll never know. I was so enamored by the Statue of Liberty at the end of the movie that I couldn't stop talking about it. We were exiting the theater, having the best time, when we saw Grandma leaning against her Chevy, arms folded. Furious!

How dare Mom take us without her permission! Or something like that. She would have driven us if Mom had asked. But Mom pointed out to Grandma that she was usually at work around this time, which made Grandma's face go from scarlet to purple. The upside, we saved on bus fare that day. The downside, Grandma was onto Mom. To be fair, Mom said that Grandma was menopausal and not herself, which I learned is an older womanly affliction.

When Dad returned to North Carolina, we had a family meeting. He said were moving back to Georgia. Hurray! Only, we weren't going home. He had sold the house. We were starting over. Mom was in shock. She was glad to go back to Georgia, but not happy *her* house was sold. They never told us what happened. It was another secret for the adult vault. We were assured that our toys, bikes, and possessions were in storage. We'd get them back when we had a place to put them all. We just had to be patient.

Ratings System

In 1968, the MPPC (Motion Picture Production Code) was replaced by the movie rating system.
The original (1968-1970) movie rating:

G—General Audiences, no restrictions, or warnings (family)

M—Mature Audiences—parental discretion advised (from 1970 to 1972 this was changed to **GP**)

R—Restricted—persons under 16 not admitted, unless accompanied by parent or adult guardian
(1970-1972 persons under 17 needed a parent or guardian to accompany them)

X—explicit sexual activity, adults of 16 years of age or older only, no exceptions even if accompanied by a parent
(1970-1972 changed to admit no one under 17 years of age)

https://www.historyandheadlines.com/november-1-1968-how-do-movies-get-their-ratings/

Movies were starting to change and not in a safe way for my teen brain. Well, everything was.

We really didn't have a direction for our lives other than returning to Chamblee. It was a time of uncertainty. Sadly, Dr. Martin Luther King, Jr. was assassinated not long after we got back. Robert Kennedy was assassinated as summer began. I remembered JFK's death and I didn't know why all my heroes were dying.

I was heartbroken by MLK and RFK's deaths. They were people I wanted to be like. The news gave me the impression that they were like Jesus. Helping people. All people. Which is what I thought hippies were all about. Peace and love. I could not understand why anyone wanted to hate or hurt others?

I didn't like anything about 1968, the Vietnam War, all the assassinations, or moving. I deemed it the worst year of my life. I had also formed an opinion that Democrats, of which Mom was one for sure, were careless people. Not that Mom was, but how did Kennedy Democrats keep getting killed? It was troubling for a young Catholic mind. I concluded that Republicans were much better at keeping their people alive. Like a kid who puts a *kick me* sign on your back for laughs, I felt there was something not right with the Democrats. Then Mom reminded me that Abraham Lincoln was a Republican, which made me feel good, then bad because he'd been assassinated, too!

The Democratic candidate after RFK died was Hubert Humphrey. All I could think was Humpty Dumpty. We know how that ended, so I became a Nixon girl. Our teachers wanted us to experience voting, so we had a school presidential election. We didn't study the candidates or politics, we just had a day to made paper signs to hold up one day, then we had our vote the next day. Would our vote be like the real election? Nixon vs. Humphrey. Nixon won the kids' vote, probably because it was easier to spell his name correctly. And Nixon won the national election, too. Hurray! That's all there was to it. We moved on.

There weren't many (or any) women on the nightly news programs. We watched Walter Cronkite and Huntley and Brinkley, newsmen that looked like principals to me. Since war and murder were the leading nightly news stories and movies were getting new ratings, what else would adults do next? Could they stop fighting? Behave? End hating? Keep their hands to themselves? They expected kids to. What about them?

My television role model at the time was the actress Patty Duke, who played dual roles on a show named for her, *The Patty Duke Show.* She played an outgoing city girl Patty Lane, as well as her twin cousin, Cathy Lane, a smarter, sophisticated girl of the same age. I much preferred Patty Lane. I also liked to read about Patty Duke in magazines, but her real image wasn't the happy girl I watched on television. Instead, she was pictured smoking cigarettes and wearing heavy makeup. Her role in the movie *Valley of the Dolls* along with Sharon Tate and Barbara Parkins was controversial. The dolls weren't Barbies, they were the barbiturates and Quaaludes their characters were taking. It seemed that real Hollywood people were taking strong medicines, too. Articles reported that doctors were helping their actor patients with prescribed medications, and actors were also finding illegal drugs.

I once took a digitalis meant for my great grand-mother. I was supposed to deliver the heart medication to her and wasn't listening and took the pill. Everyone was so upset! They watched me for several hours, and when my heart didn't explode, they all went back to whatever they were doing. I can't remember feeling any different.

Since the parents were home-less, we moved to Carriage Hills Apartments, a family complex. You'd think it was a campus. School buses lined up at the apartments and took a kid or two from every unit to elementary, junior high, or high school. Across the street was a Tenneco gas station that had a convenience store like none we'd seen. Kids could shop alone and buy candy without their parents hovering over them. It was like *The Jettsons*, the best version of the future! We were old enough for Mom to trust us with candy money, get on the school bus, and find our way to our classroom once at school. That's all I remember from the Carriage Hill period.

I don't recall friends, the school, or anything but the deluge of kids who went to the convenience store. The polite merchants treated us with respect by counting exact change back to us and told us they'd look forward to seeing us tomorrow. The store owners loved us. The candy vendors loved us. I loved them! The Tenneco station was heaven; school was hell.

Georgia taught reading through memorization of sight words. This meant you guessed how a word sounded by remembering a word already you knew. Terrible! I read aloud, "The monks live in a monstrosity." I guessed at the word *monastery* because I was familiar with the word monstrosity, as Mom would use it frequently when telling us to pick up our rooms. *Wrong!* The class had a good laugh. I turned all shades of blistering self-consciousness.

Reading was painful.

Did I have a defective brain? Why was reading so difficult? How did Mom do it so easily? I admired her, but I was also extremely jealous. She had just restarted her mail-order book subscriptions since her personal library was in storage. She also purchased mass-market paperbacks at grocery store spindle racks, like Victoria Holt gothic romances, as well as Michael Crichton and Arthur Hailey suspense novels. These thick softbacks were a marvel to me. I dreamed that someday I'd be able to read a whole one.

While Mom devoured 400-page novels and stacks of gossip magazines like a research librarian, I struggled to get through a few chapters of homework. I prided myself as a specialist of *Rona Barrett's Hollywood* and *Silver Screen* headlines, photo captions, and scandal snippets.

Somewhere along the way, a teacher read *Charlotte's Web* to our class. That's when I fell in love with the concept of story, story in the sense that a real girl, Fern, had a pet pig, Wilbur, with barnyard friends, among them a talented female spider, who saved him from slaughter. I wanted to be Fern. She was a lucky girl. I wasn't so fond of Templeton the rat, but I adored Charlotte. The communication between Wilbur and Charlotte kept me on the edge of my seat. To think that a small female arachnid could spin beautiful messages that made adults stop and think! That made me cry.

Inspired, I checked out a school library book, *White Bird*, told from the bird's point of view. Every night I read in bed, even finished in the allotted check-out time. Finishing was a wonderful accomplishment! You'd think I'd repeat the process and get another library book. I didn't. I savored the experience. Later this translated into fits of excitement when I went to my first Scholastic School Book Fair. Could I grow my own library, like Mom? It was a great idea that never caught on.

While Mom had her strengths, she also had her weaknesses. The New Math meant nothing to her. She knew her multiplication tables, and she could add, subtract, multiply, and divide whole numbers, but that was it. We were to pay attention in school or call a classmate for assistance. The phone could be used for that.

If the New Math had been taught in the film *2001: A Space Odyssey*, we might have had a fighting chance of knowing something about it. This was the kind of film Dad liked. Mom, not so much. A lot of adults didn't understand the Stanley Kubrick masterpiece. However, I did. It was my Georgia education experience. In the beginning, God made apes, cave dwellers, and teachers. As society evolved into families of astronauts (who moved a lot), things got busy. Somewhere along the way, young space travelers were educated by the super-computer HAL. HAL was responsible for the New Math, I was convinced.

HAL would not "open the bay doors" of knowledge for me. Instead, I had to venture untethered into deep space and find the answers for myself. But I did not. I knew it would be eons before help would arrive and I'd be an old decrepit woman in the silence of an empty intergalactic classroom. The baby at the end was just a slap in the face. Like a baby can do these math problems! Get your parents to help you with your homework!

Thank goodness, we were only to have half-a-school year in Chamblee when Dad called another family meeting. The parents were incredibly happy. A little too touchy-feely for my tastes. What was the news? Tada! *We* were being transferred. Again.

We. Not, *he.* Significant difference. Dad said we could vote to either go back to North Carolina or move to Florida.

Florida! We'd still be going to North Carolina for Christmas.

So, we moved to Brandon, Florida. I think they spelled it wrong. It should have been called Branded. Brandon was a cow town. There was nothing there but a strip center, Pioneer Plaza, with a new J.D. Bradford store, Publix grocery, a card shop, etc. Dad would work out of this location and be home every night. *Every* night. Every *night?* *EVERY NIGHT!*

We kids had concerns. We saw Dad a lot more at the apartment. He was traveling less, but still gone a lot. Realistically, we were Mom's scene-changing crew. Mom was our production manager. We ran lights, props, and struck the set for all of Dad's entrances.

Depending on where we lived, he either had a front or garage door entrance. Lookouts would check from the front drapes to see if it was curtain time. Occasionally, one of us would miss our mark, and another crew member might slink in to do a quick change-up of toys on the floor to toys under the sofa while the leads, Mom and Dad, performed their opening embrace.

Could we do this seven days a week? Matinees and evening performances? It was a tall order! Thankfully, the Sir Laurence Olivier of credit management often bypassed Act One and Two and made a grand entrance into Act Three when his children were in bed.

He was home early every night the week of July 16th, 1969, for the Apollo 11 launch news and eventual moon landing. This was family time. We kids were to be calm and watch the television as a family. *Watch!* Especially July 20, 1969, when the astronauts took their first steps on the moon. I really didn't want to pay attention, but Dad insisted. I wasn't allowed to go out to the front yard and squint at the moon and look for the lunar rover. I had to stay put.

To give you a little perspective, we lived on the opposite coast of The Kennedy Space Center. We never went to see a launch or other touristy things related to the space program. We did watch *Star Trek* and *Lost in Space*, though. Franky had an astronaut helmet J.D.

Bradfords sold in the toy department, which was as close as we'd ever get to the space coast. When Neil Armstrong's said, "That's one small step for man, one giant leap for mankind," it was one small step for the Knight family, and one giant leap for Knight time (meaning we watched in real time). I was glad Dad made us sit there.

When Dad wasn't at home, the store was his home. Basically, the store was his real home, and our house was the place he managed. He was the boss of both. He could slip out the back door of either. There wasn't any retail competition in cow town other than one family saddle store boutique. Scotland's sold quality saddles, pricey western clothing, and boots. The Sears catalogue was the closest thing the locals had to selection. Mom was all about quality over quantity, and Scotland's earned her respect. Buy better was her motto. To appease Dad's loyalty to his employer, we explored Scotland's only if Bradfords didn't carry the same item.

If you really wanted to do some serious shopping you went downtown, the locals said. This was Tampa, more like uptown to me, another planet in the Florida solar system as far as we were concerned. Greyhound went to Tampa. The county bus, if there was one, was not taken by anyone we knew. We walked to Pioneer Plaza from our house. A cab to Tampa was not affordable.

Once we were moved into our new house, we learned that Sea-Monkey number four was due in autumn. My birthday candles had paid off! Mom said that regardless of whether she was having a boy or girl, the name would be Dana. I didn't like the name, but okay. A sister named Dana was fine. The only Dana I knew Mom liked was actor Dana Andrews. I didn't know of any actresses or characters named Dana, so I figured she knew something I didn't.

Since Mom and Dad were getting along a little too well, she started going to the beauty shop on Fridays to get her hair set in an updo that she called the Juliet. I had never seen nor read Romeo and Juliet, but the style looked more like Ava Gabor's *Greenacres* hairdo.

On beauty shop days, I would sit in the shop with Mom. The boys were given change to buy Mom a sandwich and themselves something to eat. They had to wait outside the beauty shop and try to control themselves. I usually drank a soda and ate potato chips while pursuing the salon's magazine stack. There was a Miss Kitty (the saloon keep in *Gunsmoke*) beautician that did Mom's hair regularly. Kitty knew of Dad, since Bradford's back door faced the front door of Kitty's salon. She'd ask Mom about Dad the entire time she was doing Mom's hair. Mom listened and said little. If Mom said anything, all the hair stylists leaned in. Dad was a dreamy downtown man to these hairspray-ingesting babblers.

Since we were not cow people, but suburbanite transplants, Miss Kitty and the girls liked to mutter about the goings on of a bar up Highway 60 heading out of town. It was a watering hole for vendors and professionals passing through and of whispered, townie rendezvous. We, or rather Mom, smiled weakly at the information. It sure seemed like the ladies wanted to lure Dad to the lounge for a high ball. Whatever a high ball was.

One Friday I asked to have my hair done like Mom's. Miss Kitty squealed. She would do my hair. She whispered a lot of questions in my ear. I didn't understand what she was talking about. So, I did what I normally did when an adult talked to me: smiled, nodded, shrugged, or stared. Kitty talked nonstop, snapping her gum, and cackling at her own jokes while lacquering my hair into a tornado updo. This didn't resemble a Juliet. Mom looked elegant. I looked scary.

My brain froze at the sight of chimpanzee ears. *My* chimpanzee ears! *Did I always have these? Where were they all this time?* My mind raced. I realized that Mom had hidden them under pixie cuts, long hair, and braided pigtails down each side of my face. I had never worn a ponytail! She knew!

With such large ears, you'd think I could hear for miles, but the holes inside my head were rather small. Turns out, not long after witnessing these head wings, the school alerted my parents to a suspected hearing loss. Schools did a lot of simple testing, which also included eye exams. As a result, I wore glasses (when they weren't lost or destroyed. I left my first pair of glasses on the driveway in Charlotte, and Grandma ran over them). Anyway, Dad had to take me to an audiologist in Tampa.

During the audiologist visit, I was given a hearing test. Hermetically sealed in a soundproof room with a sportscaster's headset, I was to repeat words and phrases. Then I was to repeat words and phrases I could barely make out above loud static blasting simultaneously with the dialogue. This was followed by a hand-raising beep test. I was to raise my hand when I heard a high-pitched beep with and without static. It got terribly confusing. What I had not told the doctor or my dad was that the emergency broadcast signal screeched in my ears all day, every day. I assumed it was the same for everyone. The test beep at times was masked by the ringing in my ears. I raised my hand at confusing intervals. *Was that a beep or the ringing?* Hand up. *Or was the ringing echoing the beep?* Hand partially up. *Could the beep or the ringing really last that long?* Keep hand up. The doctor looked concerned. Keep hand down.

I didn't know my hearing was different. I don't recall when the ringing started. It was determined my hearing loss came from chickenpox or measles and I had simply adjusted to it.

Emerging from the depressurized capsule, the doctor strapped a pair of hearing aids on me. I could hear people everywhere! People talking throughout the office, and beyond the room we were in, to the elevator, the people in the elevator. I shook my head, no. I didn't want hearing aids. Dad assured me it was okay to have hearing aids. Though he may have been relieved to not be spending an enormous sum, he was more than willing to do so. Dad told Mom I needed hearing aids. I said I didn't want to hear *THAT* much! Now, it would've been cool to spy like Agent 99 on *Get*

Smart, but I definitely would have lost, damaged, or stuck them in a drawer. I was not a careful child. Mom would not have demanded I wear them or maintain them, and would have trusted me to do so.

I imagined what hearing aids would look like on chimpanzee ears. My towering updo received the compliments of everyone in the salon while my brothers laughed hysterically and tapped on the window. I really wanted to punch the crap out of them. The ladies shooed them off. By the time I stood, I was shoulder high to Mom, who had her own hair height. Thankfully we took a cab home. It was for the best. We might have caused collisions if drivers saw my pillar of hair. It was a bit of a struggle getting in the taxi.

Dial M For Murder

> *Over two grim nights in Los Angeles, the young followers of Charles Manson murdered seven people, including the actress Sharon Tate, then eight months pregnant. With no mercy and seemingly no motive, the Manson Family followed their leader's every order—their crimes lit a flame of paranoia across the nation, spelling the end of the sixties.*
>
> *—Chaos, Tom O'Neill*

It was a *Fright Night* like most Fridays in our house. We were lined up on the couch watching movies and eating Jiffy pop° Popcorn while waiting for the 11:30 monster flicks to begin. The Tampa CBS affiliate news anchors concluded their Friday broadcast eating and yammering about the sponsor's Cuban food as horror fans patiently waited for a night of terror. About the time the flan was featured, Mom complained she was having worse cramps. *Cramps?* We observed her discomfort. Did nothing. Kept watching television. She said she needed to call Dad. We shrugged. Sounded like a plan.

As Mom grew increasingly stressed at her inability to reach Dad, we remained focused on the closing credits of the news. It was late and Bradfords wasn't open, so where was he? He often did work late and didn't answer his office phone after hours. So, she called another retail wife. This woman's husband worked for Dad. He'd find him. We nodded reassurance to Mom.

Within twenty minutes, Mrs. Fitzsimmons, a fine Catholic woman, drove to our house to get Mom. Mr. Fitzsimmons still hadn't located Dad. The Fitzsimmons had to get someone to watch their children, while Mr. Fitzsimmons searched for Dad.

Mrs. Fitzsimmons drove Mom to a hospital in Tampa (where the televised Cuban restaurant was) to give birth to Sea-Monkey Dana. We waved off the moms, promising to stay inside, not fight, keep the doors locked, go to bed after the movie, and tell Dad where Mom was. *There was no way we'd unlock a door at midnight, especially during a horror movie.* Besides, remote controls had not been invented, and a pause button didn't exist on the television. Regardless, we were way too chicken.

There we sat, the dark house illuminated by the den's television. Mom was fine. She was always fine, well, other than whatever made her sick enough for us to go to North Carolina, but other than that, we were not worried. I had not even considered that Dad might become a widower father like all the shows we watched. Our mom was a trooper!

An hour into *The Black Cat* (Boris Karloff and Bela Lugosi) we heard the garage door. *Dad.* We didn't move. A garage door opening was usually a warning for a one-minute drill, shoving clutter under things to make the house appear clean. Would Captain von Trapp expect us to be in bed?

Dad walked in and we told him in unison, "Mom went to the hospital to have the baby."

He yawned. "Tampa General or St. Joseph's?"

"St. Joseph's."

He said, "Tampa General?" yawning louder.

"No! St. Joseph's," we shouted.

"Tampa General," he said matter-of-factly.

After about five more Tampa Generals we realized Captain von Trapp was not his usual self. But he took our suggestion and left. Turns out he'd broken down on a cow town road and was stranded for hours. Since cell phones hadn't been invented then and roads were less traveled in some areas, he was at the mercy of a mechanically inclined motorist to rescue him.

Being clueless about safety, we encouraged him to leave immediately and see Mom. Since we weren't the type to put ourselves to bed, we slept with the television running until Dad came back after sunup, looking crumpled and a little refreshed. We had a sister! He went to bed.

Several hours later we got in the car and headed to St. Joseph's. We were going to see Dana. Dad gave us the highlights. Our new sister had had the umbilical cord around her neck on her way out. Once untangled, Mom had a transfusion. Dana had a lot of hair. She was beautiful.

Sidebar: I hold the record as the only perfect birth.

Once at the hospital, we were not allowed to see Mom or Dana, because of the age restriction. Stupid hospitals. So, we sat in the waiting room thumbing through magazines awaiting Dad's visit to conclude and to get more updates. I picked up a *Life Magazine* with a photo of a man sitting next to an open door that had "pig" written on it. I read that his wife was actress Sharon Tate, eight months pregnant, who had been murdered. Sharon Tate wasn't ringing a bell. This was horrible. I had never seen anything like it in a magazine.

This was worse than Jayne Mansfield being beheaded in a car crash with her kids asleep in the backseat. Hollywood deaths were rare. This was scary! The husband was director Roman Polanski. The word "pig" was written in someone's blood. I read the entire article, we were there that long. I was totally disgusted. Why would someone do that? Why would the husband pose with a bloodied door? Could it be his wife's or baby's blood? I was thinking way too much. There was something seriously wrong with this man!

We didn't know about graphic violence other than war stories. We watched *Alfred Hitchcock Presents,* his films, *The Birds, Vertigo, North by Northwest* and even *Psycho.* But nothing we watched was as horrific. *Life Magazine* was scary. Why did Sharon Tate and her baby have to die? Thankfully, our Mom and baby sister were safe in the hospital.

Two days later Mom came home, and we met Dana.

Mom said, "She's Bailey."

I say, "Where's Dana?"

Mom said she didn't look like a Dana. Well, that threw me. I was prepared for Dana, boy or girl. I didn't know Mom could change her mind. She and Dad always told us to make up our mind, choose, and that's it. Live with it. Why do *they* get to change their mind?

"Bailey from *It's A Wonderful Life?*" I asked.

Mom nodded. "Sounds cute, doesn't it?"

"But that's a last name, Mom." I liked that she was getting creative, but it was a bit puzzling.

"A last name is another way to honor a family line," she said.

I looked at her with uncertainty. "We aren't related to George Bailey. He's not real. At least Clark Gable was a real person."

Mom thought a moment. "Moms and Dads give their children names based on their family, intuition, and other things." I'll admit Bailey was better than Dana, so I just accepted her logic. But it still seemed terribly contradictory that grownups got to change the rules to suit themselves.

Thus began our lessons in how to care for a baby. It started with a cloth diaper service and samples of something new, disposable diapers. Regardless of which diaper you used, you had to stab a big fat diaper pin through the layers of folded fabric or plastic cotton-filled disposables and close the pin. Diaper tape had not been invented then. Diapering sounds simple, but I feared I would stab my hand.

Unfortunately, Bailey learned the hard way. I decided to take a short cut and just jab the pin into the diaper and quickly snap it shut without putting my hand inside. Bailey started screaming and physically shake-crying, as babies do when pinned to their own diaper. I looked in. I wanted to pass out. I had grabbed her skin in the diapering process. I popped the pin open and pulled it out immediately. Mom came running in, and I showed her the pin mark on Bailey's hip. It sounds horrific, but somehow there was only redness and no blood. What a terrible big sister I was!

We would soon discover Franky was much more proficient at diapering. I chalk that up to his working with tools on model planes and ships. The diaper pin was an instrument Franky mastered. I, on the other hand, decided to mummy-wrap Bailey's bottom in two diapers with two pair of rubber underpants to create a ball of absorption. Mom was not impressed.

Bailey was barely two weeks old when *Butch Cassidy and the Sundance Kid* screened at the Tampa Theatre in downtown Tampa. Mom really wanted to see this movie!! She convinced Dad to take us all. Dad was a western fan, so it was a no brainer. Once popcorn and sodas were acquired at the concession stand, the family headed to the balcony. The second-floor women's restroom had a sitting area outside of the lavatories.

That's where I spent time one hour and fifty minutes with a well diapered Bailey, thanks to Mom.

I rocked Bailey and every so often walked up the steps to a landing that led to the balcony seats. This was not a great idea knowing how clumsy I am, but I watched the entire *Raindrops Keep Falling on My Head* bicycle scene as I rocked her to the tune. I didn't care if I missed most of the movie, I had a new sister—a real baby that was mine!

I showed her off to women who came into the restroom. They were concerned that a newborn was at a movie. Which I found silly. Surely it was better to babysit at the theater versus leaving an inexperienced eleven-year-old home with an infant. If we'd known Bailey would sleep the entire movie, I could have held her in the theater. Instead, we bonded in the sitting room of the historic 1926 theater.

Before the year was out, Bailey went to lots of movies. We saw *Anne of the Thousand Days* with Geneviève Bujold as Anne Boleyn and Richard Burton as King Henry VIII. This was another movie where Mom said I reminded her of the lead, Anne—in appearance and stubbornness. Anne was beheaded for refusing to give King Henry an annulment. He wanted to remarry and have a son with Jane Seymour, thus robbing Anne's daughter Elizabeth from future queendom. I liked that analogy, but the beheading part was a little concerning.

Mom saw me as strong-willed, though merging Anne and Scarlet was a mixed message. Scarlet was independent and spoiled, Anne trapped and willing to die. I would have much rather I resemble a mischievous Hayley Mills in *The Trouble with Angels* or *The Parent Trap*.

Speaking of girls, boys were in the majority in our neighborhood. My best friend in elementary school was the principal's daughter, Jeannie, which was equal to knowing Caroline Kennedy in my view. Her father looked like President Johnson and his office was equal to the Oval Office.

Jeannie and I laughed a lot. We liked happy, cheerful pop like *Sugar, Sugar* by the The Archies, *Good Morning Starshine* by Oliver, *Build Me Up Buttercup* by The Foundations, *Get Together* by The Youngbloods, *Aquarius* by The 5th Dimension, and I was obsessed with *This Magic Moment* by Jay and the Americans.

It was also about this time my Mom gave me a pamphlet about menstruation.

Mortifying!

The pamphlet had illustrations of women's internal organs, the uterus, and ovulation cycle. Yuck! I read a few paragraphs and stopped. I had seen Mom's lavender Kotex boxes in the bathroom cabinet, always hidden. Tampons had not been invented then, or weren't well known, so I'd soon be sharing her Kotex supply. The pamphleteer, Mom, asked if I had questions.

I said, "No." Mom looked relieved. She didn't want to discuss it any more than I.

My first period was a big secret, like the time I punctured my shoe. Only I didn't use Absorbine Jr. on myself but made my own maxi pad. I didn't want to use any of Mom's Kotex, in case she was keeping count. Everything was hidden. I hand washed my own underwear, took out the bathroom trash, anything I could to keep from telling her. By the third month I was on board with using her supplies. We didn't discuss it. I hated everything about becoming a woman. Nonperiod weeks were the best.

At about the same time, the world was becoming obsessed with Charles Manson, the leader of his own cult, The Manson Family, who were arrested for the murder of Sharon Tate, her friends, as well as others. The magazine article I had read on our hospital visit to see baby Bailey was now a mystery solved. He had yet to go to trial. But the definition of hippie changed from peace and love, to drug addicted killers, and Charles Manson was their leader.

It was a negative time. Thankfully, our subdivision was full of positive young families who were more outgoing than ours. A neighborhood mom, Mrs. Lewis, created a talent extravaganza to keep every kid on our block busy that summer: the Mrs. Lewis Variety Show.

To be clear, there were no summer camps in cow town. Cow kids had lots of extra chores over summer break. Everyone made do. The public pool was an option. Mom didn't swim but allowed us to walk to the pool since we knew how to doggie paddle. She had a baby to care for, and we enjoyed the independence of going to the pool via the cow pasture less traveled. The resident bull used us for workouts. He was docile in the morning, but by late afternoon our chlorine-soaked bodies had his nostrils flaring. He chased us far enough to show us who was boss. We had to avoid getting bull crap on our shoes. Mom made us throw our shoes away if we stepped in dog crap, so bull crap was definitely going to be an issue. We didn't touch any crap, other than Bailey's.

Anyway, Mrs. Lewis made us practice songs, dances, and skits in her backyard for months. No one was allowed in her house. We could go home for lunch, but it was chop, chop and back for the second half of the day. Hers was an outdoor training ground. She and her clipboard agenda determined all the acts, costumes, decorations, flyers, tickets, and refreshments. We were to practice being audience members as well as performers.

As an experienced third place award-winning first grade lip sync artist, forced to sing *A Spoonful of Sugar* for real, I was determined to lip sync this time. Can't remember what. Franky was a talented artist and drew the stenciled flyer as his contribution. He refused to perform. Adults in the neighborhood received mimeographed invitations for the big performance. Copiers and consumer office supply stores were not invented then, so duplicated flyers were mimeographed.

Our stage was the cement patio behind the Lewis' house. We entered the stage from their sliding glass door, the only time we were allowed inside. The curtain was drawn between acts. The audience paid admission and brought their own lawn chair. Little kids were admitted free if they were accompanied by an adult.

Admission proceeds paid for a big ice cream party hosted by Mrs. Lewis and any leftover money was sent to World Vision charity. The show was a hit.

Mrs. Lewis got us through the summer. So did the twin brothers who started a garage band and performed most evenings. The twins were that good. I often walked Bailey in her stroller at the exact time I heard them warming up. The brothers were much older than me, and yes, I developed a crush on one of them. I was their groupie. Bailey happily bounced to their evening performances.

Her first amazing skill after crawling was to turn on my record player, toss a 45-rpm at the spinning turntable, push the needle across the unseated record, then bounce happily to the skipping noise. Cute became maddening. If I left my room for a soda, went to the bathroom, or answered the door, the sound of little hands and knees slapping across the floor would waft through the house as Bailey made her way to opportunity. I didn't have extra furniture to hide my record player or albums from the baby disc jockey. It all sat at the foot of my bed on the floor.

In fact, when placed on the floor, Bailey would crawl all 2100 square feet to see what everyone was doing. At times we parked her in the stroller. We eventually got her a walker, but she advanced so fast that we had a challenge keeping track of her. At one point, Dad got her one of those metal kiddie cars for us to drive her around the house. It sounds silly, but her toy became ours. She'd crawl her diaper clad self beside one of us pedaling her car across the terrazzo floors. Thankfully, a distant cousin sent hand-me-downs for her because she grew so quickly it was difficult to find things that fit her. She was a big girl, not a fat baby, but a large, strong girl who was perfectly content to be bounced on one of our hips. Eagerly awaiting the return of all three of us each afternoon, Bailey was Mom's sidekick as she watched soap operas, did dishes and laundry, and wrote letters to the aunts and grandmas.

Franky and I were in junior high school by then, and Clark still in elementary. For me, seventh grade was a bit like entering the *Twilight Zone*. Imagine if you will, hundreds of blue one-piece (snap-up) romper-fitted girls charging onto a junior high school's blacktop to perform the sport-of-the-day, followed by a naked crowd scene. To be clear, I had no interest in physical education, ever. I had barely passed the President's Physical Fitness Program in elementary school. I couldn't run fast enough, jump high enough, or tumble over my classmates without flattening them. As a menstruating teen, I was also learning that my body didn't sweat. It swelled. Other girls sweat; I bloat. Not breaking a sweat to gum-snapping whistle-blowing female coaches was a sign of laziness. No matter how red my face got, if I didn't drip sweat, nothing counted.

This summed up my whole public education experience. Nothing counted. Moving from school to school, my prior transcripts didn't translate with the next school's administrators. They'd huff and sigh. "What did they teach you in North Carolina, Georgia, or wherever you come from?" Educators were adults who were allowed to insult you for your own good. They called it "teaching moments."

Nude shower time was unlike anything I could image a school legally requiring. It was unfathomable that hordes of unfamiliar girls of all shapes, sizes, and ages would take a compulsory communal shower (naked) for a grade. Sure, I'd changed clothes around friends before, no big deal. But undressing around a hundred plus girls in a sweaty smelly locker room with no privacy? I'll take an F. I was warned that I could fail a whole grade if I failed gym. Parents and teachers seemed to think if they told a kid they would only flip burgers and pump gas if they failed school, it would incent them to work hard. I would gladly flip burgers than jump into a giant shower of multiple shower heads with a bunch of strangers. There were a couple of shower stalls with no doors for girls on their periods, *like that was somehow private*. I didn't look at anyone or want them to look at me. Of course, there was always someone who would shout "pervert," accusing another girl of staring at her. I would have preferred they blindfolded us all.

My parents raised us to respect privacy and not enter a room when someone was changing and to knock at the bathroom door to make sure no one was in there. But now in junior high I was expected to be okay with *naked fest*. So, I wore my underwear and bra into the shower, kicked my feet around and wrapped up in a towel to present myself for a grade.

Whistles were blown. Screams of, "Listen up ladies, if we have to go over this every day we will! You are to take off your gym clothes, which includes your bra and underwear, enter the shower, wash the sweat off, towel up and get in line." This was followed by another loud whistle, which sent me into sensory overload. My ears rang twice as loud when I heard, "Line up!"

I was a D student at best in any subject, no matter where I went to school. These tough broads weren't going to crack me. I tried to please them, though. Hid my bra straps, wrapped the towel tight. They'd open my towel with a yard stick to see if I was wearing anything, then diss me. Reminding me I was failing gym. *Fine by me.* After towel inspection, it was time to dress quickly and get to my next class before the bell rang.

My first junior high shower and gym class, I'd worn a handmade broomstick skirt Mom made me. She was not a seamstress. She'd been inspired by some pretty fabric she saw in Bradfords. I thought it looked good for a homemade garment, and I didn't have any prejudices about clothing or brands. Mom had gathered the red and white flowered print to my waist size, hand-sewed a band around the top, and hemmed it herself as part of my school wardrobe. It was one handmade skirt, and I was fine wearing it, until I realized I had to step into the skirt and close it with a large safety pin because Mom didn't know how to make buttonholes or add a zipper. A diaper pin would have been much more secure. Mom had made the flap a little too wide, which meant my underwear might show if I didn't tuck my shirt down completely.

I was shaking, trying to beat the clock, and mortified I might not close the safety pin completely and have the whole skirt fall off as ran. The bell rang. Off I raced, holding the side of my pinned skirt, along with my purse and notebook. I stopped in a restroom and triple checked myself and got to class late as I did regularly after every gym class. Of course, the teacher thanked me for finding time to attend class and marked me tardy. Tardy was a Knight trait. They should be thankful I was there.

Franky and I never talked about how the boys behaved at shower time, not that I wanted to know. We both hated junior high.

The following summer we moved again. Dad's job was not secure. We felt bad for him. The retail chain was shedding locations, jobs, inventory, and closing the cow town store. This was fine by all of us. We loved our house, but we'd had already cycled through holidays, aunt and grandma visits, several grades, garage bands, Clark and a friend nearly burning down the woods behind our house, raising three pet rabbits in an ice-cold air-conditioned house, later cats, being chased by a raging bull, and the beauty shop rumor mill.

Next stop: another apartment building, this time in Dunedin, Florida.

Dunedin is on the beach side of Tampa Bay. We moved into a two-story, two-bedroom townhouse, where the boys had one room with two twin beds and Bailey in her crib. The boys had talked Mom into allowing them to have a snake in an aquarium—in their bedroom! Where our little sister also slept.

Clark's prior snake incident (with his best friend) was to smoke a snake out of a pine-needle strewn hole. The result? The pine tree went up in flames like a roman candle. Image two boys running in slow-motion from an explosion, the likes of John Wayne in *Hellfighters*.

Clark promised Mom he'd keep a lid on the aquarium and an eye on his serpent. The snake had other ideas. It escaped. We checked on Bailey a lot, worried she might get strangled in her sleep. I don't know why we didn't keep the snake downstairs. Likely because Mom didn't want to see it. We also had a pair of kittens that we hoped might find the snake. But they escaped, too, out the front door and onto the grounds of the complex. We never saw them again. We were terrible pet owners. I'm pretty sure the rabbits died from pneumonia due to Mom's need for blizzard-like temperatures in the house. Animals that escaped were better for it.

Talk about a tight squeeze. The other bedroom had my and Mom's two full-size beds and chests of drawers. We could barely turn around. There was a lot in storage. When Dad was home, I'd sleep on the downstairs sofa.

The Dunedin complex had a mix of nice younger families and troublemakers. I was turning thirteen then and the object of every young mother's attention. "Do you babysit?" they'd ask, my first foray into entrepreneurship. Once they learned that I had a two-year-old sister, it was like the *Good Housekeeping* seal of approval. Of course, I was experienced. "How much do you charge?" they'd ask.

Mom encouraged me. She babysat in her teen years. This was a chance to make some serious pocket money. We all got a little allowance from Dad, but I now could earn my own money to spend or save. I also was also a lender. Mom and the boys sought loans from me until Dad got home.

I opened my first savings account with my babysitting income. There was a bank within walking distance, and if Mom and the boys asked early, I could spot them a few dollars before I deposited it all. Once my bankbook hit $100, I needed a serious goal. I was friends with a girl who lived a few apartments over. Mary had a horse that we brushed often. The stable was a block away, sandwiched between the apartments and a residential neighborhood.

When she rode her mare, I shoveled its manure and refreshed its hay. I wasn't experienced at riding, saddling, or physically coordinated, so shoveling was something I could do. It was a lot more interesting than sitting at home. Mary's parents encouraged us to go to the stable often. So, I made a goal to buy a horse. It was peculiar how I lived in cow town and never encountered a horse, but when I moved to a beach community, I cleaned a stable regularly. Nevertheless, I bought the newspaper each weekend and studied the want ads. I wanted to learn how much horses were going for.

Since kids were aplenty at the apartments, I was growing my horse fund in leaps and bounds. Bratty kids were my specialty. I sincerely didn't know the difference between a brat and a regular kid since I lived with the slap kings. Mothers of spoiled tikes sought me from outside the apartment complex, even stalked me after school. Betty, a stocky waitress with a leathery pro wrestler tan and white, blonde hair pleaded with me to watch her kids. I checked with Mom, and she said, "Okay, just once." I had to walk to the family's house after school and before Betty went to the restaurant. The job entailed: hang out, do my homework, feed the kids, put them to bed, and when her husband Ralph came home, which would be after dark, he'd drive me home.

Their children were a pair of blondes, a girl aged four and a boy aged five. They sat on either side of me and stared at me the entire time like the children from *Village of the Damned.* I kept the television on to amuse them, but they seemed content to mind meld with one another. That might creep-out some teenagers, but I talked to them, did my homework, eventually fed them, and put them to bed. On the other hand, Ralph, the dad, really creeped me out. I recognized him from the photos around their house. He came home late, smelling like beer. A short, barrel-chested Jimmy Cagney type with nicotine-stained fingers and teeth, a rubbery sunburn, and thick curly white hair, he drove me to the apartments in his GTO convertible, top down, while the kids slept at home. He made some excuse about how much money he had on him, then gave me what sweaty cash he had in his pocket, not knowing how much Betty had negotiated. Ralph had racked up extra hours, and I wasn't certain if he or Betty were good for the balance. Once was enough.

"Stupid Ralph!" Betty cried. "Ignore him!" *Like I could.* He was my drunk ride. She begged me to come back. Please, the kids hated every babysitter she ever hired. Would I please come back!? She'd pay me more. I didn't. I followed my gut. If they had lived in our apartment complex and I had lifelines or I could have subbed jobs to Mom, I would have. But as it stood, I was in charge, and I had plenty of clients to choose from.

Multiplexes

1970s

The genius of the mall multiplex was that when families were done with their shopping, they could all go to the movies without being obliged to watch the same film. They could go to the theater "together but separately," wrote one mini-theater exhibitor in 1970.

—https://www.boxofficepro.com

Things were becoming more stressful with the parents as Dad took the couch at the apartment. I was no longer rotating with him. His first love, J.D. Bradfords, had broken his heart. This caused a strain with his second love, Mom. Since his kids were growing and changing quickly with each passing year, he questioned if we ever loved him. Rejection has a way of eating at a breadwinner. An overachiever will find fault in themselves when their employer tanks, no matter how hard they try to keep the company ship afloat. It was easier for Dad to do nothing than disappoint another group of people.

It's not like we didn't try to cheer him up. None of us really knew what to talk about. Watching television together was the closest thing we did as a family. Only now, Dad no longer demanded we be quiet. I think in some ways he felt he was a visitor in our house, and he had to be quiet.

Thankfully, the Samsons came down from Atlanta for a Florida vacation. Our families met at a waterfront seafood restaurant within walking distance of their rented bungalow. The men drank cocktails. That was a first. The kids got loud. The women tolerated it all, and it was as close to a reunion as Dad would ever have with his retail family. We all stayed the night at their rental. Bailey slept in a drawer. We kids camped on the guest room floor in between jumping on the bed. The dads snored on recliners in the living room, and the moms talked until dawn in the master bedroom. The next morning, we had a big breakfast, and it was the last time we'd see the Samsons. Mom and Yvette stayed in touch through letters.

Soon Mom and Dad found an older home in Clearwater behind Sunshine Mall. Dad had peace of mind knowing his wife and children had access to stores and lots of movie theaters. There were three movie theaters in a five-mile radius, aka walking distance, if we lacked cab fare. The Trans-Lux at Sunshine Mall, the Capitol, and Carib Theatre on different sections of Cleveland Street. I still don't know how we had the money to do any of the things we did. We nickel and dimed everything. We would go to the Ranch House Restaurant and split a plate of fries and a couple of sodas, taking up a whole booth and spending extraordinarily little. It was one way we could stay in air conditioning and keep our sister contained.

The Trans-Lux theater was at the mall. We always showed up after the movie started (old habits die hard) and watched the last half of a feature and waited for the next showing to see it from the beginning all the way to the end again. We had no other place to be. It all came together when you saw the first half.

When multiplexes began to open and lines wrapped around the complex for screening times, we were totally mystified. We'd never been in a line. They had always let the lady with a cab full of kids and a purse full of coins in to see the movie when she arrived.

Movies became increasingly explicit in the 1970s, with more nudity, language, and violence. As a teen who had grown up with little exposure to these, the messages were not of interest to me. I'd much rather deal with the subtle *dead mother* scenario that screenwriters and directors relied on than male dominance in graphic detail. One particularly eye-opening film Mom and I saw was *The Prime of Miss Jean Brodie.* This was the first time I saw frontal nudity of a young woman who was a student *on screen*. I had already experienced frontal nudity in the junior high showers but watching it on the big screen with Mom was gross.

The student in the film was having an affair with her adult male teacher. Mom didn't bat an eye. She stayed with the story. She was always transported by whatever was on screen, in the moment. I was back into full *Hawaii* mode, but not crying, mostly looking away and closing my eyes. If Dad were there, he would have marched us both out. I would have preferred that to sitting through the movie wondering why Mom wasn't uncomfortable. I never thought of walking out on my own. She would not have minded. She'd expect me to wait in the lobby. Missed opportunities.

Mom counted me as a full-fledged woman by this point. I wasn't so sure I wanted to be in the club. Biologically, yes, but I didn't want to see sexual stories. She'd raised me on fairy tales. I suppose *Cinderella's* stepsisters could have seduced the handsome prince, but they didn't. So why did growing up require milestone reveals? Just give me the pamphlet. *You're 10, you're getting boobs soon. You're 11, you're going to be sharing your mother's maxi-pads soon. You're 12, you're going to get naked with your classmates for a grade soon. You're 13, men are looking at you for sex—well, maybe.*

We didn't cuss as preteens, but there was a cuss word I had taken a liking to. Up to this point, I can't recall my parents saying anything more than *damn it.* However, when I heard Ali Macgraw say "bullshit" in *Love Story,* I took notice. It was heartfelt and playful coming from her. Compelling. *Maybe I would say this in the future?* I wondered if Mom would. It was also the first time I remember a young woman dying in a film versus being the well-loved *past tense* mother whose photo graced a bedside table, or portrait overwhelmed the family's fireplace mantel in loving remembrance of her sacrifice in birthing an heir.

Love Story, for me, packed a memorable punch in my development. The couple, Jenny/Ali Macgraw and Oliver/Ryan O'Neal were students in love. Unlike *The Prime of Miss Jean Brodie* where the girls were younger and promiscuous, this couple was smart, fun, and opposites in many ways. Ali Macgraw's unforgettable line, "Love means never having to say you're sorry" melted my heart. I loved Jenny and Oliver together. She should not have to die. I loved them!

Thankfully, broadcast television was the exact opposite of film in the 1970s. Light-hearted family comedies and variety shows lifted our spirits when movies brought us down: *The Brady Bunch, The Partridge Family, Mary Tyler Moore, Sanford and Son, The Carol Burnett Show,* and a Saturday morning favorite *Lancelot Link: Secret Chimp.*

Unlike our other houses, which were always built to the parents' preference, the Clearwater house was used. It had three bedrooms, one bath, a kitchen, a dining room, a living room, an entrance room off the sliding glass door porch entry, and a guest room/converted garage. Ever the realtor at heart, Mom hoped to turn the guest room into a rental. That room had a small staircase, a drop ceiling that deceptively covered attic rafters and a rear exit into the laundry room. The laundry room had a toilet, sink, shower, and exposed attic rafters.

The conversion was my room. Its composite foam ceiling tiles looked solid until there was a storm. At first gale, the tiles would lift, giving a haunted house vibe. *Sometimes* the tiles settled back in their original place Not only did the ceiling lift, but at lights out, roaches stormed the room from the attic. I don't mean a roach here and there. I mean flying, swarming, crawl-all-over-you cockroaches and palmetto bugs. Bailey and I would get up, screaming and swiping them off. I'd spray the room again. It was a nightly event. Leaving the light on helped, but it was hard to sleep. I stupidly thought I could win the war of the roaches.

The entrance to our house had a screened porch door, followed by a sliding glass door with a latch lock and top pin to secure the main house. Since we had three mostly inoperable wall air conditioning units, we kept the front sliding glass door open to bring air into the house from the porch.

The Manson Family could have slaughtered us on a trial run. We were easy marks. If murderer(s) did approach from our driveway, they would have gotten in and out with ease. However, if they approached from the front yard, they'd have become victims of our sandspur mine field. More about the yard later.

School during this period was the same as any other. I had no clue what they were teaching. We did a mix of public and private school. For one year, Franky and I walked to St. Cecilia's Catholic school both ways. It was about 1.5 miles. We stopped every day at McDonald's to split an orange soda and a small order of fries. Clark walked to a public elementary with neighbor kids in the opposite direction. Bailey stayed at home with Mom. I don't know how we afforded McDonald's, much less the tuition. That's one of those parental mysteries. I think we were part a *class availability* thing. We were moving down the economic food chain and tuition forgiveness or partial forgiveness was a thing. Or maybe Mom had called her Vatican connections.

This was an enjoyable time for Franky and me. I liked wearing a uniform. It was like being in the Brownies or Boy Scouts. Girls could wear cute hair bands, barrettes, and some jewelry, but that was about it. We couldn't wear makeup, though most of the popular girls found ways to keep their cosmetics near translucent. The nuns took pointers.

I was still sure, back then, that I was going to Hell for something. Catholic guilt was real in pubertal days. I wrote a lot of poems from the point-of-view of the unborn—my inner genetic egg or Sea-Monkey memory was working overtime.

In our eighth-grade Catholic reproductive class that was not sex education, because Catholics didn't discuss sex education, I got overwhelmed thinking about conception while staring at the poster of a baby in the womb. The teacher told us that at five or six weeks you can hear a baby's heartbeat. Suddenly the menstruation pamphlet became a cartoon in my mind. I started thinking about all the blood in my body and the fetus swimming around. There was a lot of blood and other liquids in there, including orange soda. I gagged. The room felt warm. I yawned loudly. I put my head down on the desk and felt my body go limp and tumble out the desk opening. The desk wobbled back to its upright position once I was on the floor. Next thing I knew I was smelling rubbing alcohol.

The teacher had retrieved a rubbing alcohol bullet from the class medical kit, broke it open, and was rubbing it under my nose. I could see through the slits of my eyelids that the boys in my row of desks were trying to look at my underwear, which was exposed when my uniform skirt flounced. I contemplated faking a coma. Could someone just carry me out? I did not want to face my peers. Eventually, I allowed them to sit me up. The girls looked concerned. The boys were snickering.

A boy and girl escorted me to the school nurse. I called Mom. She and I agreed I was fine. I would walk home later with Franky. I didn't want to talk about it with anyone, and I didn't. However, Mom consulted her medical encyclopedia of mostly tropical diseases to rule out Elephantiasis, Malaria, and the Plague. If I wanted to know more about conception, *the women's disease*, I could check her resource.

Clark didn't like public school any more than I did. He was across town in South Ward Elementary. There wasn't enough stipend for Clark. He got his turn at private school once Franky and I moved on to Middle School (which was retitled from Junior High). When Clark did attend Catholic school, he was unimpressed. The teachers and principal had changed and were more militaristic. But thankfully he and Franky were no longer fighting regularly.

Eventually, Mom tried to steer Dad toward entrepreneurship. She wanted a book shop or rental property. Dad rolled his eyes at a bookstore. Anything artistic was a losing proposition in his mind. There could only be so many Vincent Van Gogh's, Harry Belafonte's, Sophia Loren's, Orson Welles, or James Michener's. Therefore, a bookstore was just one big inventory problem. There would not be enough bestsellers to pay the rent.

Mom was more excited about real estate, so the bookstore discouragement didn't bother her so much. She found a builder, a corner lot in Safety Harbor, and told Dad they could afford two duplexes. She really did her homework. Dad was impressed and agreed. She planned and kept him in the loop. He managed the banking. If all else failed, we'd live in one unit and rent the other three to pay the mortgages.

The first few months after the duplexes were completed only one unit was rented. Dad panicked and sold them. Part of the profit went to a boat. Mom rolled her eyes. She had an opinion that anything recreational would be expensive. There was no upside in a boat, motorcycle, convertible, or camper. Now they paid slip rent, boat repairs, and gasoline to joyride.

Since Dad was still out of town most of the week, the boat became a summer hangout for my brothers and me. We walked the five-mile hike each way to the marina when our bicycle tires were flat. By the time we got to the boat, we'd sit there, eat snacks, and Clark would fish. Often, we pretended we lived on the boat and sometimes played *Gilligan's Island.* I was Maryanne, Clark was Gilligan, and Franky was the Professor. It was a fun time, apart from the neighboring boat owners who hassled us. They didn't believe our dad owned the boat. It would be twenty questions and warnings that "you kids" better not…

After several hours of leisure, we'd walk home. Our yard in Clearwater was an obstacle course of sand spurs. Sand spurs are pea-sized thorny tumbleweeds. Think thumbtack balls spread across a sandy weed-choked front yard. You couldn't go barefoot. Plus, we had a spike-tipped yucca plant curbside, called The Impaler. No one parked there. Ours was the most dangerous yard in the neighborhood. It's obvious the previous owner had control and privacy issues. There was no lawn to mow, though the boys did crank up the mower and chopped spurs for something to do. They wanted to mow other people's lawns to fund comic book, model plane, and candy purchases. I struck a deal with the boys to bid on the mowing jobs they'd mow. I got paid a third for landing the job. One elderly neighbor, Mae, didn't have much grass. She had sand and weeds. She wanted the weeds pulled and was willing to pay $40! That was a lot of money.

I paid my brothers $10 each, and we all pulled weeds until the streetlights came on and continued in the dark by a streetlamp. Mae told us to go home and finish the next day. I wanted to be done and get my money. Mission accomplished. We finished that night and came back the next day to inspect. It looked like nothing had been done. Had the weeds grown back overnight!? I suddenly felt like con man Harold Hill in *The Music Man*. Thankfully Mae was elated. She thought we had improved the appearance of her yard. Lesson learned. Don't mess with a happy customer.

So, with renewed confidence, I solicited Mae's neighbor, Hilda. A tiny German woman of eighty, Hilda trimmed her grass with scissors. Her yard was totally overgrown. I figured this was an instant score. I didn't realize that her knee-high grass made her feel at home. I thought the place looked abandoned. But soon, I pictured young Hilda running with Maria von Trapp along rolling hills of tall grass in the *Sound of Music*. Hilda didn't want me or anyone to touch her finely curated field. Mowing was mass destruction by her definition.

Instead, she asked if I would consider being a server.

Hilda hired me to serve and wash dishes when she hosted friends. Hilda cooked and employed a chef to create authentic German delicacies. The day of, I would set up card tables with tablecloths, flowers, china, silverware, and ringed linen napkins. I was to hang back and await Hilda or the chef's orders. These were semi-formal occasions but seemed formal when contrasted with Knight family Christmas dinners. Our family had all the same dining paraphernalia, but Hilda's etiquette elevated mealtime to event status. As a server, I wore a dress, closed-toe flats, and a provided bib apron. I poured water, tea, and coffee, brought out servings, picked up dishes, and was not to socialize with Hilda's friends. When everyone was gone, I washed dishes. It was an hourly position and Hilda paid me before I went home. She never invited me to sample her food or take a leftover home. I was a contracted hand. No fraternization. I felt respected, responsible, and adult. We were neighbors from a distance. She was independent. Drove herself and was quite popular in her German American community.

Besides my kitchen-maid income, we also sold the grapefruits that grew in our backyard. We didn't like grapefruit, so it was easy money to bag up our fruit and take it to the produce stand across the street. It also cut down on the fruit rat population. We never thought about chopping down the grapefruit trees. Instead, big game hunters, Franky and Clark, shot the rats that escaped into our well house with their Christmas BB guns. The boys would stand at our back sliding glass door and hold the dead rodents by their tails until we screamed and locked the doors. Totally disgusting.

Vince, the produce stand owner, was a nice Italian man more than willing to buy a bag of grapefruit every so often from his best customers. And we were the best. We were *need* shoppers. We always needed something, mostly a gallon of milk. It was Mom's security thing. She needed a full gallon in the fridge before by night-fall. Think Joan Crawford's *No wire coat hangers*, only replace it with *There must be milk!*

Another money maker that kept us all busy was potholder looms. These red plastic forms and multicolored cotton loops were sourced from McCrory's and Ryan's Gems and Junk in the mall. Sharing caused fights, so Mom got us each our own loom. When we had a few dozen ready, Mom sent us door-to-door to sell them. Our neighbors were all good sports but could only use so many potholders. Beyond a few streets, the potholder demand dried up quickly. It was not a great revenue stream but good for a flash handmade gift when our traveling aunts and grandmas were in town.

All these communal moneymaking escapades were separate from my horse fund. I was still saving and reading newspaper ads regularly, envisioning my mare living in the de-ratted well house like *Mr. Ed.* Then Mom sat me down for a heart-to-heart. If there had been a pamphlet for letting me down easy, she would have given it to me rather than say what she had to say. "Everly, you are not getting a horse."

What!?

She said:

1. I couldn't afford to stable a horse.
2. I couldn't afford to feed a horse.
3. I couldn't afford to travel to wherever the horse was boarded.
4. Most importantly, I didn't like to ride horses.

STOP!

While she was correct on every point, Mom also was a *National Velvet* fan. Surely, she understood that if twelve-year-old Elizabeth Taylor could steal America's heart as girl jockey Velvet Brown, I had a right to become a real horse-girl! How did this Elizabeth Taylor analogy fall flat? She was firm. *Nope.*

So, I invested in the next best thing. Siamese kittens. I spotted Siamese cats for sale in the livestock ads, set an appointment, and even paid the cab fare for all of us to meet the Siamese breeders. Think Disney's "We Are Siamese" *(if you please)* pair. Certainly, one horse was equal to two *Lady and the Tramp* songsters.

I named the girls Ginger, and Taffy. Bailey called them Gin-gu and Bappy. They were the cutest, most adorable kitties on the planet. But the novelty wore off quickly as we discovered they were indeed Siamese (if you please!) and would howl alternately for 24 hours. They never seemed to sleep or move. Their favorite spot was a wicker chair on our front porch. Their staggered "Yeow," "Yeow," went on for hours. All day, all night, unless they slept or ate. "Yeow."

Like Disney's Si and Am, Ginger and Taffy took control of not only our house, but our neighborhood. About this time, my brothers complained that it was unfair for me to have two cats and they didn't even have one between them! So, Mom funded their pet purchases. *The copycats!*

We all piled into a cab—Me, Mom, Franky, Clark, and Bailey—and went to the SPCA.

The cab driver knew us and waited with the meter off. Franky picked a white mouser and Clark a gray tabby. Upon adoption, the boys' cats alternately howled loud obscenities. They must have seen our family on a wanted poster. No one thought to bring a carrier.

Clark's gray tabby yowled loud enough for all the kennel inmates to hear. A brash *I'm getting the hell away from these people* howl! The volume and intensity grew as he and Clark exited the shelter. The moment the cab's back door opened, the meter started. Everyone was in but Clark. Franky's cat was fine. Clark's gray tom gripped the rubber molding on the door frame as Clark yanked him. The cat wouldn't let go. We were all spellbound. Where would these claws go next? No sooner had Clark unhooked him than the animal's needle-sharp teeth went for his hand. Our younger brother let out a terrifying scream and released his cat to freedom. Injured and sad, Clark sobbed. The meter was turned off.

Mom and Clark went back in and picked out a yellow tabby. The SPCA didn't require another adoption fee. Once home, the boys gloated. They were all great mousers, the boys and their cats. Not a terrible thing. The boys were better pet owners than I was. I sold Ginger and Taffy to good people, real cat lovers who would care for them better than I would. Then I opted for two docile Guinea pigs that I named Alexander and Aristotle. Bailey called them Anger-ganger and Doodle-dot-tell. Bailey loved all our animals.

It soon became obvious to me that I was more of a transactional livestock broker than a pet owner. I grew bored with A&A, realizing they looked like rats without tails. I sold the Guinea pigs.

In time I would discover fashion at Sunshine Mall's Stuart's apparel. I then invested my hard-earned money on 1970s fashions, everything bright and polyester.

Dad was not around as much once we moved to Clearwater. The routine weekend stayover was now a few hours on Friday, and he was gone. Mom made Bailey my roommate to entice Dad to stay Friday and Saturday. It didn't work. They decided to break up. We all just accepted the fact, like our cavities.

Mom knew she needed more money than Dad could supply. So, Mom applied for a waitress position at a white tablecloth destination restaurant in downtown Clearwater across the street from the Capitol Theatre. She'd seen the *Help Wanted* sign when we were exiting *Deliverance*. Her server uniform was a matronly black-and-white striped short-sleeve maid garb. Occasionally, she would send a cab to get us when she was working and treat us to dinner. We were Bailey's babysitter and each other's keeper. She made generous tips, and friends, and became independent.

Once the divorce went through, we were unchanged. It was sad. Dad still visited and did things with us, but not as often. He paid child support, the mortgage, and the power bill. But knowing his credit management discipline, he was probably relieved to have structured debt as it related to us. He would eventually find Sally, who would become his world. He never stopped being Dad, he just stopped being a live-in.

Grandma June would return every six months or so on a Greyhound when she got fed up with Richard and would return to him when she got fed up with us. The other grandmas and aunts kept the United State postal service busy with letters to Mom. Mom, of course, kept in communication with them, Uncle Link, and Father Mallard.

As we teens were maturing and developing our own interests, I found I could no longer watch the horror films that were being produced in the 1970s. Mom could. I could not. Especially after watching *The Exorcist!* It was too Catholic, too scary, and I had no intention of letting the devil converse through me. Not that I thought he could, but why take any chances?

Instead, I became a musical fan. *Jesus Christ Superstar* and *Godspell* suited me fine. After all, if I did decide to risk my life and have children someday re: the menstruation pamphlet/reproduction class, I wanted to be sure my eggs were exposed to upbeat entertainment.

The End.

Art References

Cover art by Sherman Kew

Sherman Kew—A transplant from southern Maine, Sherman Kew moved to California after graduating from the Film/Animation/Video department at the Rhode Island School of Design (RISD) '03. Currently, Sherman resides in Peachtree City Georgia with his family drawing storyboards for TV shows and films and writing children's books and novels.

www.shermankew.com
www.instagram.com/shermankew

Womb art by Kathy Powell

Kathy Powell—Kathy Powell is a Florida transplant who was born in Ohio originally. Kathy says, "I have known Emily for many years, and I have always treasured our friendship. I am honored to create something special for this book!"

She loves to do Random Acts of Kindness—aka known as painted rocks. She loves to doodle on rocks to bring joy and love to others. Her "weapon" of choice is Tooli-Art from House of Santorini. Being retired has many benefits she believes, and art is one of them!

Public Domain Art

Inspiration for womb art—public domain https://me.me/i/ wanna-see-something-cool-did-you-know-that-your- GrandMother-19961399

Sea-Monkeys—Public domain Pinterest.com and Google. com

The Day The Earth Stood Still poster—https:// freeclassicimages.com/movie-posters-t4.html

Cyclops art—Public domain https://www.pinterest.com/ pin/568086940500212499/

Spray Tan—Public domain https://www.pinterest.com/ pin/214484000974712418/

Bestoink Dooley—https://1.bp.blogspot.com/_2f- w1dyS2ip4/TNlXYEDJB2I/AAAAAAAAAJY/ iR0r2M6amKw/s1600/bloodmountain2.jpg

Jonathan Frid, Dark Shadows—Public domain https:// en.wikipedia.org/wiki/Barnabas_Collins#/media/ File:Jonathan_Frid_Barnabas_Collins_Dark_ Shadows_1968.JPG Photo

UNC-TV—Public Domain—UNC-TV Presents A look back at the four most popular children's programs from the 50s, 60s, and 70s. https://l.facebook. com/l.php?u=https%3A%2F%2Fvideo.unctv. org%2Fvideo%2Func-tv-presents-stay-tuned-boys- and-girls-promo%2F%3Ffbclid%3DIwAR3ZAkjm Cum_migzw6S7u4WccGH3OAMbFMtTgP4K2ZB7 D5XqrNR5m-N9bhg&h=AT26pQO5YlkCqXe1UV 7DOEUCmsHtKAYRMWWoxyUWwcSjgoAYEqyN 1eOueYHLZmVhAvzlF6awh03HBFxiaGT8gsbes6Er qWDii0oVE74AUzCI9d6W-eFm8vciXBYjHIFf65ky- FeK9dBfjLsexw&__tn__=%2CmH-R&c[0]= AT1ojhngAMZCcX8pYwY7ZGvST9nqdWL I1V_-rQjPjYsLMo_TI45mjhBs8p131FiUA8yuPU QKPNOfgxOXi1Cje_6cEfpZt1NMHc-NlkJNA- ikrAVZt7v7MblSlBuXH57OPVEb

Acknowledgments

Thank you to Lisa DeSpain for saving me again! She has now edited two novels and formatted all my books. I'm truly lost without her. Thank you also to Sherman Kew for the incredible cover art. Sherman is an amazing storyboard artist for film and television. You'll find his contact information listed in the art references. A big thank you as well to my cover designer Claudia at Labelschmiede.com. She has created six book covers for me and restored my grandmother's photo that is featured on *Until We Sleep Our Last Sleep*. Consider checking out her website. A big hug to Kathy Powell, who created the womb art that begins the book. Kathy and I have been friends for a long time having met at our employer Valpak. I really needed Kathy's piece to jumpstart me. It turned out fabulous! Special thanks again to Tom Hillman at tomhillmannmediadesign.com, who created and manages emilyskinnerbooks.com.

To my friends who read, write, assist, and/or encourage me: Grethen Wells for incredible feedback,

Terrie Wolf, Beth Swain, Regena Stefanchick, Becky Marble, CJ and Gregg Fisher, Suzy Rodenbach, Howard and Lot Whittington, Robyn Fairbanks, Susan and Ernie Zager, Elle Thorpe, Roxanne Smith, Judi Burten, Carrie Vanerio, Roberta Terranova, Theresa Moser, Judy Roe, Joyce Huslander, Susan Logsdon, Kim Salter, Marcia Engle, Marylou Bourdow, Kathy Durnell, Elaine Duval, Val Ross, Tracy Brandt, Doris Hurst, Jennifer Prange, Kathie Fahey, Glenn Ireland, Lori Garside, Muriel Savino, Peggy Sheffield, Peg Connell, Kathy Durnell, Laurie Williams, Ramon Mendoza, Pat Lynch, Pam Corkum, and Sheila Ramler. You each provide me motivation to keep in the game. To Tampa Theatre Marketing Director, Jill Witecki, it is wonderful to know you keep a cherished landmark relevant. I sincerely appreciate your friendship. To Natalie Symons for being a great table neighbor at book signings events.

To family members who support me: Tom Skinner, Barbara Williams, John and Kathy Williams, Blair Skinner and Caitlin Poley, Marquel and Drew Rogers, Ellen Williams, Cecilia Garrison, Robin Williams, Kathleen Sims, Mark Williams, Ruth Skinner, and Selena Sieb. Thanks for the love! Forgive me if I've missed anyone.

Acknowledgments

Last, I am forever grateful to the following libraries, bookstores, gift shops and clubs for hosting book signings, and author events, and/ or stocked signed copies of my titles.

Portkey Books
Safety Harbor, Fl

Books At Park Place
South Pasadena, Fl

Sunshine Book Co.
Clermont, Fl

Annette's Book Nook
Ft Myers Bch, Fl

Unbound Bookery
Lakeland, Fl

Wilson's Book World
St. Pete, Fl

Stillwater Books
Pawtucket, RI

My Favorite Things
Dunedin, Fl

Barrel of Books and Games
Mount Dora, FL

Safety Harbor Public Library
Safety Harbor, Fl

OXFORD EXCHANGE Book Fair
Tampa, Fl

Beach Art Center
Indian Rocks Beach, Fl

Cooper Memorial Library
Clermont, Fl

Clearwater Alumnae Panhellenic Fundraiser

Clearwater Public Library
Clearwater, Fl

Fieldstone LFL Bookclub

About the Author

That time I trimmed my bangs for photo day.

Emily Skinner lives in Tampa Bay, Florida with her husband, Tom. In addition to writing, she also enjoys traveling, visiting local museums, growing sunflowers, and collaborating with their daughters, Marquel Skinner and Blair Skinner, on their film and acting projects.

Other Books by Emily W. Skinner

Hybrid Medical Thriller/Southern Noir
by Emily W. Skinner
Mind Hostage

Romantic Suspense Novels by Emily W. Skinner
Marquel (Book 1)
Marquel's Dilemma (Book 2)
Marquel's Redemption (Book 3)

Booktrailer:
Marquel book trailer on YouTube—
featuring actor Eric Roberts & Marquel Skinner
www.youtube.com/watch?v=6e6O7iYqeVQ

Young Adult Novels by E.W. Skinner
St. Blair: Children of the Night (Book 1)
St. Blair: Sybille's Reign (Book 2)
St Blair: The Diary of St. Blair (Book 3)

Historical Nonfiction by Emily W. Skinner
Until We Sleep Our Last Sleep:
My Quaker Grandmother's Diary of Faith and
Community Amid Depression and Disability
The Diarist: A companion book for your inspired thoughts

Short Memoir by Emily W. Skinner
Master of the Roman Noir

Coming of Age Fiction by Emily W. Skinner

The Movie Queen

To connect by email:
www.emilyskinnerbooks.com

Follow Emily on:
www.facebook.com/emilyskinnerbooks
www.instagram.com/emilyauthor
https://www.goodreads.com/author/show/6982753.
Emily_W_Skinner

To connect by snail mail:
Emily W. Skinner
PO Box 8590
Seminole, FL 33775-8590

Reviews and ratings are appreciated!